The Renovation

The Renovation

Gladys Whitlock

Lobathian Publishers

The Renovation

This book was originally published in trade paperback by iUniverse in 2003

First Lobathian printing in 2010

For information
LobathianPubs@aol.com

ISBN: 978-0-9821370-6-2

Printed in the United States of America

For Doris and Lorraine and all the other women who have found the courage to reinvent themselves.

CHAPTER ONE

White lightning snapped instant pictures of whipping trees against a background of boiling dark clouds as they blacked out the last feeble rays of light. Gusts of wind buffeted the small green car, threatening to jerk the steering wheel from Katherine Gardiner's hands. Then in sudden fury the threatening storm exploded through the darkness. Hard driving rain slammed against the windshield and almost stopped the wipers. In moments, rushing water covered the highway, wiping out the distinction between the narrow tarmac and muddy roadside. Automatically, Katherine drove slower and slower, picking her way through momentary seconds of blindness after each brilliant flash, searching for a place to stop and wait out the turbulence.

Inside the car she was protected from nature's excesses, but there was a burning storm churning within her, veiling a full awareness of the weather. Every thought and emotion was directed inward, magnifying her sense of injury. Smoldering resentment masked fatigue and blurred the endless miles that had rolled beneath the tires. Struggling with outraged pride and humiliation, her main emotion centered on revenge. Over and over, all the way from California to the outskirts of Baltimore impotent plans chased themselves through her mind. "He'll be sorry. I don't need him. I can take care of myself."

A tremendous crash of thunder directly overhead startled her into full awareness of the turbulence raging about her. The violent downpour blurred everything beyond the circle of her headlights and brought a little stab of fear. What if this wasn't the right road? She hadn't checked the map since breakfast, but she was sure she had memorized the route. The road sign had been glaringly bright at the last intersection, but now all she could see through the curtain of pelting rain was the shadowy outlines of trees and bushes along the gravel bank. Driving slowly, peering into the dense darkness, she had almost decided to go back and find the motel she had passed on the main highway when her headlights picked out a mailbox lettered "Patrick Gardiner." It was a peculiar sensation to see her family name beckoning out of the dark, almost as if someone had said, "You're home!"

She turned into the muddy driveway and the car sloshed alongside the house to a graveled space at the rear. There was a wide back porch with three steps gathered in a rectangle of light shining from a window. In the cold wet darkness, all the light in the world seemed to be coming from that one window.

Wearily, Katherine switched off the ignition and lights. As she did so, the kitchen door opened and a tall, gray-haired black man appeared. He came down the steps unfolding a large umbrella and extended it protectively as he opened the car door.

"Mrs. Gardiner?" he asked.

"Yes." Katherine's lips felt stiff as she smiled. "You must be Fred."

"Yes Ma'am. Won't you come in the house, Mrs. Gardiner?"

"Gladly, but I have to get my suitcases out of the trunk first."

"I'll do that, Ma'am. No need for you to mess around in this rain," he said, a wide grin showing a mouthful of white teeth in the dark face.

"Okay," Katherine said gratefully. "Thank you." She handed him her car keys and he escorted her to the open door where a rather plump, smiling black lady now waited. Clad in a white denim apron over a dark dress, she gave an impression of neatness and efficiency.

"Mrs. Gardiner, this is my wife, Lily."

"Welcome, Mrs. Gardiner"

"Thank you, Lily. I'm certainly glad to be here."

Lily stood aside for her to enter the huge old-fashioned kitchen.

The heart of this room was a massive range providing a huge expanse of cooking surface and a slight smell of wood smoke. In addition to a large oven across its front there was also a warming oven across the top of the high back. From the top of the warming oven to the sturdy claw feet it was decorated with tarnished scrollwork. It suited the huge proportions of this room built in a more generous era than the present, while it made the cheap chrome table and chairs appear a century out of place.

There were ragged, stained shades at the windows with faded calico valances. The wallpaper, too, was faded and torn where it showed between ancient oak cupboards, which reached to the high ceiling. In some places many footsteps had completely erased all signs of the floral pattern from the old linoleum. The room was depressing, yet still carried a hint of a gracious past, like a proud dowager ignoring her rags.

A hearty aroma of hot coffee arose from a blue enameled percolator puffing softly on the stove. Shedding her jacket, Katherine gratefully accepted a cup of the strong brew but she was too tense to sit.

"Thank you. Maybe this will warm me up. I didn't know it got so cold here at this time of year."

"This is unusual," Lily assured her. "It's because of the rain. This is only the middle of summer so there'll be lots of hot sultry weather yet."

Cup in hand, Katherine walked around the old Gardiner family home, inquiringly opening doors and peering into cupboards.

"That's the pantry," Lily told her when she looked into a cold empty room lined on both sides with dusty shelves and storage bins.

"Good night!" Katherine exclaimed. "I've been in grocery stores that weren't much bigger than that."

At the back wall of the kitchen three steps led to a small landing with a handrail on the left and a door on the right. Curiously, Katherine opened the door to expose a narrow stairway curving up into the dark. She quickly closed it again on the musty, stale-smelling air that flowed down the stairs and noticed that Lily hurriedly backed away from it.

"That's the back stairway, Ma'am," Lily explained, wrinkling her nose as if the smell was offensive. "The front stairs go up from the parlor."

Katherine was beginning to wonder if she might have to deal with outdoor plumbing when she found a bathroom behind the next door she opened. Obviously a makeshift arrangement, the builder had installed a washbasin, toilet and claw-footed bathtub on a section of the porch. Then he built walls around them and cut a door through to the kitchen. The old porcelain was cracked and stained and the metal fittings rusted, but someone had made a valiant effort to clean the place. To her surprise, everything worked, even the hot water tap. Apparently, there was a modern water heating device tucked away somewhere.

As she moved around, Katherine became aware of an appetizing aroma coming from the stove area.

"What do I smell?" she asked Lily

With a pleased smile Lily opened the ornate warming oven and showed her a small casserole. "I thought you might come hungry," she explained.

"How thoughtful of you. I didn't realize I was hungry until I smelled it, but now I'm starved."

Lily started as Fred bumped through the door with several suitcases. She seemed relieved to see him.

"Why don't you let Fred show you where the bedroom is," she suggested eagerly. "I'll set your supper out."

"Sounds good," Katherine agreed, wondering why the smiling black lady seemed to be a bit hurried. For no apparent reason she appeared nervous and ill at ease, yet glad to welcome a new owner of the house.

Picking up her jacket, Katherine relieved Fred of the smallest of her suitcases, and followed him out of the kitchen. Their footsteps echoed across a shadowy formal dining room, which was separated from the huge parlor by a wide stairway. Dim light rays from the parlor barely revealed a graceful curved banister and the first few steps. Against the back lighted effect the steps appeared to lead up into blackness that seemed almost dense enough to be felt.

The light on the other side of the stairway came from a single unshaded light bulb in a tarnished bracket mounted on the far wall. It shed a glaring light over a parlor furnished with yard sale discards. A lumpy couch stood next to an equally lumpy overstuffed chair. A heavy wooden kitchen chair sat on the other side of a coffee table, which was supported by a lath splint wired to one broken leg. Limp flowered cotton drapes tried to provide a bright touch, but they were too short for the immensely tall windows. Because they had been strung on a cord about ten or twelve inches below the top of the frame, the whole effect in such stately windows was totally incongruous.

After a moment's hesitation, Katherine followed Fred across the room into what apparently had been a library. To her relief, this room was a great improvement over the others. It was smaller and contained a large carved wardrobe and a dresser matching the bed and end tables. There was a wooden rocking chair, lamps and a small braided rug on the floor. Fred and Lily had converted it into a comfortable bedroom. A few old magazines scattered on the bookshelves added a lived-in look that contrasted happily with the echoing emptiness of the rest of the house. Fred dropped her suitcases at the foot of the bed and closed the faded chintz drapes.

"I'll have a fire goin' in a minute, Mrs. Gardiner."

"Thank you." She shivered a little. "It's really chilly in here."

He opened two little black iron doors set in the wall and revealed a neat pile of firewood stacked on the small grate, ready for lighting. At the touch of a match, flame climbed greedily through the kindling to lick the logs. In minutes, Katherine could feel the heat reaching out to her.

"How nice! I never saw a fireplace with little doors set in the wall like that before."

Fred adjusted the damper. "It's a Ben Franklin stove, Ma'am. Every room has one. Guess it was the only way they knew to heat a house when this was built."

"It must have taken mountains of firewood."

She had seen pictures of similar fireplace stoves in magazines recently. The antique nostalgia had returned them to favor as a decorating item, but this one was smaller and protruded only a few inches from its brick setting in the wall. She was appalled at the thought of how much wood it must have taken to keep such a huge house warm with all those little fireplaces. She suspected they didn't keep the house very warm either in really cold weather, but she was glad they hadn't been replaced with central heating. Such a sentimental thought was totally impractical but at the moment that bright little fire seemed to be the only inviting thing about this place.

Waiting while Fred added several more logs to the fire, she examined the dark woodwork of the bookcases and window frames. It was badly in need of refinishing. This house had been old when she was born. It had seen Civil War uniforms, hoop skirts and candlelight. She knew its age from Charles' correspondence, but there was a vast difference between a cold legal communication and heat radiating from a hundred and a fifty-year-old fireplace. Long before she existed, people of another era had warmed themselves at this grate or looked out of the tall windows that reached almost to the high ceiling. Through a century and a half this house had sheltered bits of humanity and watched them pass on. For a moment fantasy gave life to the mildewed old walls, then her stomach brought her back to more earthy thoughts. She realized Fred had left and she was very hungry.

Turning to the mirror, she unpinned her hair and ran a comb through the dark waves shot with silver. She felt better when the French roll was neatly re-pinned, but the face in the mirror reflected more years than it had a right to.

No one could blame the young lawyer who thought she must be eligible for social security. He was so embarrassed when he found her to be almost ten years younger that his fumbling attempts to apologize only emphasized the point. The incident annoyed her and she had been surprised to recognize a pinprick to her vanity. She considered herself a sensible woman on honest terms with her mirror.

She was even a little contemptuous of those who were coy about revealing their age. Still, she had felt a little resentful, almost insulted. The mirror reflected a mocking, slightly crooked smile. She sighed aloud. Perhaps she had been complacent instead of honest. The overhead timbers creaked and she had the oddest sensation that a sigh of sympathy echoed softly across the ceiling. Startled by her own imagination, she threw a sweater around her shoulders and hurried to the kitchen and away from her thoughts.

In spite of its air of decay, the warm kitchen offered a cheerful welcome. A small bowl of yellow chrysanthemums decorated the table where Lily had laid out a simple meal. Katherine was touched by the extra thoughtfulness.

"I really appreciate this, Lily. I'm so tired I probably would have gone to bed without eating anything."

"You're welcome, Ma'am." Lily immediately reached for her jacket on a nail by the door. Fred was gone and she kept looking around the room uneasily. She seemed eager to leave; yet she hesitated.

"Will you want me early in the morning?"

"No, I'm tired enough to sleep late, ten will be early enough." As she spoke Katherine realized she really didn't know what arrangements the estate lawyers had made with the Parmenters. All she knew was that they were the caretakers living in an apartment over the garage. It was obvious that they considered taking care of her to be part of their duties. Clearly, Katherine needed to have a talk with the law firm as soon as possible.

Lily still hesitated by the door.

"Is everything all right, Mrs. Gardiner? Do you want anything before I leave?"

"No," Katherine said, "everything's just fine."

"You're not afraid to stay here alone?"

Now that it had been put into words, Katherine knew the big empty place did make her a bit nervous, but she shook her head.

"There's nothing here that would tempt anyone to break in."

Her smile was returned hesitantly. "No Ma'am. Good night."

Lily's manner puzzled her, but the excellent meal immediately claimed Katherine's attention. The only sound was the clink of her knife and fork on the plate and the occasional creaking of the house in protest of the dropping night temperature. She was surprised at how quickly the food disappeared when there was no other person to talk to. In the quiet, the full realization of her situation began to grow.

Charles had offered her anything in his possession for his freedom. She remembered wanting to throw his offer back in his face but common sense said she deserved something from their years together. Defiantly, she chose the one thing she knew he considered worthless, the house he had just inherited in Maryland. It was as far from California as she could get. There would be no gossiping friends or pitying relations to watch and wonder if she could handle life by herself. Also, it offered a gratifying conviction that she really wasn't taking anything from Charles because he had never owned it.

The executor's notification had been extremely brief, stating only that Charles had inherited a large property with an architecturally sound house on it. Until she actually confronted the reality of her footsteps echoing through this derelict monstrosity, she had remained optimistic. It's an architecturally sound white elephant, she thought sourly. A fortune would be necessary to bring it into this century, and all her furious pride had allowed her to accept was half of their modest savings account. In this condition, the place was obviously not rentable and probably not sellable. A tiny thread of panic pushed at the edge of her consciousness and she ate a little faster.

Katherine came out of her abstraction to realize her plate was empty and that she had eaten too much. She looked around for some place to store the leftover food and found an old-fashioned icebox. It smelled a little musty, but it was clean and the ice chamber was full. It would do for now. She rinsed her few dishes and left them to dry on the wooden drain board.

Since there was no heat in the bathroom, her bedtime preparations were confined to washing her face and brushing her teeth with little wasted motion. As she reached to pull a cord dangling from the light over the stove, she remembered the fire. It had burned down to gray-edged coals. She refilled the firebox from a carton of split logs by the stove, replaced the lid, and closed the draft and damper.

"That should hold it until morning." It was the first time she had spoken aloud for an hour and her voice echoed against the high ceiling. A pull on the cord overhead brought darkness. Her steps echoed loudly as she walked toward the shaft of light from the parlor.

As she passed the bottom stair, a noise came from up there in the dark and Katherine felt a prickly sensation on the back of her arms and neck. Involuntarily, she quickened her step and almost ran into the light. When she stood in the full glare of the bare bulb, common sense reasserted itself and she realized the place was almost certain to have mice. It made her angry that such a tiny thing could so easily alarm her. There was just something about being alone in these shadowy rooms that touched primitive fears she thought had been left with childhood. Why there were so few light bulbs when the house was obviously fully wired for electricity was beyond her. The first thing in the morning she would buy a bushel of them.

She looked back into the dark dining salon and listened. The only sound was her own breathing. Reason insisted she wasn't afraid.

She was a grown sensible woman, a grandmother. But when she turned out the light on the wall, reason had no part in Katherine's haste to enter the bedroom and close the door behind her.

The fire in here also had burned low and she shoved several logs in on the coals. Pulling the little wooden rocker close to the fireplace, she switched off the lamp and sat watching the flames curl around the new logs. As her muscles gave to the hardness of the chair, she wondered how many other tired people had rested here in its body fitting curves. Warmth seemed to soak in through her skin and bits of glancing light touched the walls and made the room less somber. Shadows swallowed the ugly stains of age and only an ancient beauty of line and form remained in the soft hearth-glow. The same blurring effect touched a tight core of despair that had been growing inside her. The weird fancy came to her mind that this house had seemed like a dead shell when she entered it. A house without people dies in spirit long before its structure crumbles into the foundation. There was new life radiating from that flickering embryo in the fireplace.

As Katherine grew comfortably drowsy, she was aware of a slight easing of her depressed mood, of a returning belief that she could cope. Many women her age had faced a blank future and filled the years with furniture, no, with accomplishment. What made her think of furniture? She couldn't afford to furnish those huge rooms, even if there was any purpose in doing so. Vaguely amused at her wandering thoughts, she willed her mind to make a plan for future action, but her thoughts refused to be pinned down. It didn't matter. Decisions about the future could wait; she was too tired tonight.

"Like Scarlet O'Hara, I'll think about that tomorrow." It seemed an appropriate comparison in the surroundings. Her head drooped and she was asleep with the fire's warmth caressing her shins and cheeks.

CHAPTER TWO

A hard sob choked Katherine awake. Tears were streaming
down her cheeks and her throat was tight as if she had been crying for
hours. In the half-dark she didn't know where she was. When she
found the lamp and looked at her watch, it was disconcerting to find
she'd slept only twenty minutes.

What had made her cry so hard? While there had been many
tears over the past months, she had not sobbed like that before. She
had shed tears over the shock of betrayal and the fear of finding
herself on her own after so many years, but never really over Charles.
Katherine was guiltily aware that it was a long time since she had
considered herself romantically in love with Charles. Increasingly, in
the last few years, she had allowed daydreams to compensate for the
dullness of her marriage. Sometimes it was a dream of an exciting
new love, sometimes of fantastic success and independence in
returning to her aborted career as an interior decorator. Seldom did
they include Charles.

On the edge of her consciousness was a suspicion that
perhaps this whole catastrophe might be for the best. She tried
honestly to assess this reaction, to decide whether she was facing
facts or crying 'sour grapes', but her emotions were too scrambled for
clear thinking. For thirty years she had been standing on the marital
rug that Charles had suddenly jerked from beneath her feet. It was

going to take a while to recover her balance and it was not going to be easy. Now that she was free to carry out her daydreams, Katherine felt a profound lack of enthusiasm for any new romantic entanglement. She certainly didn't want to get married again and there seemed to be no place for her in the job market.

A brutally frank employment counselor had told her she was unfit for anything except domestic work and too old to learn something new. The sharp-featured lady was brusquely condescending and recommended a position as a housekeeper-companion.

"Now, we must face facts, Mrs. Gardiner," she advised sternly. "You have no training or experience to meet the demands of today's technical employment market. Very few companies will hire even a qualified employee who is over the age of forty. You are past fifty."

In the face of an attitude that insinuated a housewife must be of inferior intelligence anyway, Katherine lacked the courage to mention her desire to revive past career dreams. She had retreated from the employment office with her ego in her shoes. However, as she reflected on this additional blow to her pride, her mortification turned to resentment and then to the flaming anger that had flung her headlong into this predicament. Even now the memory made her clench her jaw in anger. Then suddenly, she knew why she had been crying. She had dreamed someone had told her to cry hard because it was the last time she could cry about the past. The 'someone' in the dream was a tiny compelling old lady who called her Katy and reminded her of her grandmother. The old woman stood leaning both hands on the curved head of a black cane, nodding approvingly at the flowing tears.

"It's the last time for yesterday, Katy," she had said. "From tomorrow, there's no looking back and no more tears."

The recollection was so vivid that Katherine quickly glanced around the room, but there was no one there. She wiped her eyes and blew her nose, firmly ending the tear storm. That's good advice, she thought, even if it was only a dream. She turned resolutely to the neglected task of unpacking her suitcases.

As she moved about hanging things in the wardrobe or folding them in drawers, her mind kept revolving about the problem of what to do with the house. There seemed to be no obvious answers, partly because she needed more information on which to base them. So absorbing were her thoughts that it was a surprise to find the suitcases empty and it became necessary to hunt for the pajamas, which had just been put away. Finally attired for the night, she propped a small hand mirror on a pillow and sat cross-legged on the bed to cream her face and brush her hair.

Busy thoughts and activity had kept the quiet of the house at bay for a while, but now it began creeping softly along her nerves. The ticking of the clock seemed to grow louder. A twig snapped in the fireplace like a firecracker. She found she was listening tensely without knowing what she expected to hear.

Finished with her hair, she moved the rocker closer to the fire and defiantly opened a novel to the place marker. It was time to get her imagination under control.

But this was not so easily done. The silence around her made a hollow sound in her ears, which kept intruding on her concentration. A draft of damp dusty smelling air oozed under the door chilling her feet and ankles in spite of the fire. Realizing she had read an entire page without any notion of what it was about, Katherine gave up. Perhaps a good night's sleep would help to regain control of her jumpy nerves.

Feeling a little foolish, she turned the heavy key in the door lock. Then she banked the fire and closed the doors of the Franklin stove. Switching off the lamp, she curled into a tight ball between clammy sheets and tried to stop shivering. Without the open fire, the room rapidly grew cooler, but gradually her body warmed under the mound of blankets. Katherine was relaxed and almost asleep when a faint unidentifiable sound from the direction of the fireplace jerked her wide awake again.

She waited. Her whole body was so tense with listening that she found it hard to breathe. Then a chill raised every hair on the back of her neck. Someone was whispering behind her–soft sibilant babble right in the room with her. Terror propelled her violently away from the weird lisping. With one wildly clutching hand, she knocked the bedside lamp across the room. Tangled in the blankets, she half lunged, half fell after it, twisting desperately to face the terror on the other side of the bed. On the far wall, a slit of cherry light danced with shadows as one gently protesting door of the Franklin stove slowly grated open, dimly lighting the room. There was absolutely nothing to be seen in the flickering glow, but the strange sounds still hung in the air. She could hear scratching like something clawing the sooty brick. A muffled, high-pitched tittering gradually faded away up the chimney. Clutching the blanket around her, she crouched on the floor waiting for the next sound, but there was only silence. After her first panic, long moments of rigid listening brought the gradual assurance that whatever had made the disturbance was gone. Ghosts and hobgoblins only existed in children's stories, she told herself. She couldn't have heard what she thought she did, yet the noise was real. She had never heard anything like it before. Finally, cold and stiff, she retrieved the luckily unbroken lamp, remade the bed and put more wood on the fire. Firmly closing the door of the Franklin stove she went back to bed and lay huddled in the dark, tensely listening for more weird noises.

CHAPTER THREE

Katherine awoke the next morning, her thoughts still searching for an answer to the sounds in the chimney. Early dawn air chilled her cheeks and brought a reluctance to leave the cocoon of blankets. She lay watching a rosy gap between the drapes grow brighter until the demands of nature could no longer be ignored. After a forced dash to the bathroom, she returned to stir up the ash-smothered coals, crammed the Franklin full of wood, and quickly returned to bed.

Watching the flames lick and grow, she listened for the muffled noises that had panicked her last night but only the tranquilizing crackle of the expanding fire disrupted the stillness. By the time the bit of light between the drapes had become blue morning sky, it was comfortably warm in the room. As she dressed, Katherine resolved not to think about the disturbance anymore. There had to be a logical explanation and she was sure she'd find it eventually.

Curiosity, along with a certain amount of bravado led her to explore the upstairs before anything else. Except for size, it appeared to be reassuringly normal. There were eight large bedrooms, evenly spaced, four on each side of a rather cavernous hall. All the worn shades were drawn. There was no furniture other than a corroded brass bedstead in the master bedroom that opened off the front stairway. The empty frame was surrounded by a great deal of broken plaster on the floor and above it, exposed laths gaped from a hole in the ceiling. It was the only unsound place she saw.

Tall windows and Franklin fireplaces gave the rooms regal character, but no hint of anything mysterious or ghostly. Katherine moved carefully so as not to fill the air with the powdery dust coating every visible surface. The windows were gray with it and dusty footprints marked her progress through the rooms. Relieved, yet a little dissatisfied, she finally found her way down the cramped back stairway into the kitchen.

Katherine found there were several boxes of dry cereal in a cupboard and a quart of milk in the icebox. After breakfast, she lingered over coffee and tried to plan as she waited for Lily. Bare windowpanes drew bright rectangles of sun on the worn linoleum. It was going to be a beautiful day, but what should she do with it? Should she make a visit to a real estate agency? They could tell her what the chances were of selling the property. First though, she had to find out exactly what she had to sell.

Charles hadn't known much about it. In the emotional climate of their breakup, neither of them gave much thought to practical things. Rather vaguely, he said there would be some papers to sign and the law firm that had traced him would give her all the details. At that time it had seemed unimportant and she had asked no questions. Obviously now, the first step called for was a visit to the executor's office. When that was out of the way, she could talk to a real estate agency.

With her first good look at the size and neglected state of the place, she had realized that selling was the only course of action open to her, and even that possibility appeared pretty slim in its present condition. She wondered if she could get it off her hands before taxes came due. Her wonderful plan of redecorating it looked pretty ridiculous at this moment.

Lily came in a little before ten and displayed considerable curiosity about Katherine's first night in the old house. Her obvious expectation of something frightening stirred resentment in Katherine's mind.

"There was some sort of noise in the chimney just before I went to sleep, but I slept very well," she mentioned with elaborate casualness. She was not going to admit that she had panicked over a few weird noises.

A moment later she knew she had misjudged the housekeeper's interest. Lily clearly was relieved that Katherine appeared unalarmed and explained eagerly.

"Oh, that was chimney swifts. They roost on the ledges until smoke from the fire starts to bother them. Then they make a big fuss moving to another chimney. There are so many of them that they crowd and push each other off the ledges. Sometimes they get pretty noisy."

Birds! The whispering of feathers brushing brick, the chattering and scratching on crowded ledges! Embarrassment warmed Katherine's face at the memory of last night's foolish panic. She was truly glad to have kept her fear to herself. It was such an absurdly ordinary explanation, and her uncontrolled imagination had made it so grotesque and frightening. That Lily's question had suggested there might be something to fear offered an avenue of self-defense, but Katherine resisted the temptation to excuse herself. After all, everyone was afraid sometimes. You couldn't go through life blaming your fears on other people.

"Have you always lived in the country?" she asked Lily.

"No," Lily smiled. "We used to live in Baltimore, but when Fred was cut to three days a week on the railroad, he went to the employment agency to find another part-time job. He was goin' crazy sittin' around the apartment the other four days. They told him all he had to do was take care of the place until they found the new owner."

"How long have you been here?"

"It's been almost a year," Lily said, "and now we don't ever want to go back to city life."

Katherine didn't answer this bid for information. She knew she would eventually have to tell the Parmenters the estate was to be sold, but decided it could wait until she had visited the estate executor to find out more about it herself.

Later, supplied with the executor's address in Lily's perfect copybook writing, a city map and many confusing directions, Katherine backed her car out of the gravel drive and headed for the freeway to Baltimore.

Finding the freeway proved no problem. Finding her way around in Baltimore wasn't so easy. She became lost several times, mostly because she was so fascinated by the city that the map did not receive proper attention. The streets were lined with what seemed to be miles of brick row houses. Their almost identical white steps marching to the sidewalk in military precision delighted her sense of order. It was so different from the sprawling individual housing of most California towns she knew.

She finally located her objective in an older part of the business district. It was a solid pile of grimy brownstone with the luxury of its own parking lot in back. Even inside, the building was dark and age-stained, yet suggested a patina of old wealth and power in it's reserved hush. A small self-service elevator lifted her to the fourth floor and she followed Lily's directions to the last door at the end of the hall. Neat black-edged gold lettering on the mahogany surface announced, KENDALL, WORTHINGHAM, & ASSOCIATES, SOLICITORS.

When she gave her name to the beautifully groomed, gray-haired lady at the reception desk, she was immediately shown to Mr. Worthingham's office. Following that sleek figure, Katherine became aware of her own appearance. It had been years since she'd been inside a beauty shop.

Her dress was too short for this year's fashion, partly because it was stretched tightly across over padded hips. Other than a little lipstick, she hadn't bothered with make-up or grooming. The realization came again that she hadn't been as honest with her mirror as she believed. It hadn't been entirely age reflected from its depths, it was also carelessness and neglect. She entered the lawyer's office feeling very self-conscious and awkward as she was announced.

Mr. Worthingham was a small wrinkled man with a central ridge of unruly white hair. The upstanding crest, along with his quick motions and frankly appraising blue eyes reminded Katherine of a Banty rooster. He politely bowed her to a seat in front of his desk, then sat and leaned back in his big leather chair.

"Mrs. Bryson will bring the documents for your signature in a moment, Mrs. Gardiner. Now is there any way we can be of further service to you?"

He gazed thoughtfully at his hands, carefully matching fingertip to fingertip as he waited for her reply.

Katherine assumed he was aware of the circumstances responsible for her claiming Charles' inheritance, but he hadn't mentioned it. If he didn't consider it necessary to refer to the divorce settlement, she certainly wasn't going to bring it up. She resented a stranger knowing her situation even if it was legally necessary.

Being ill at ease rankled, and her answer was a bit crisp.

"I would like to know the size of the estate and the terms of the will, if you please, Mr. Worthingham."

He regarded her questioningly for a moment.

"You haven't read the will?"

"No"

He flipped the button of the intercom unit on his desk. "Mrs. Bryson, please bring a copy of the Gardiner will with the rest of the papers."

"Certainly, Sir," the box answered and he turned back to Katherine.

" I believe the estate contains twelve acres of natural woodland with a small stream forming the south boundary. There are no buildings other than the house and an apartment over the garage. As you have seen, nothing has been done to the house for years, but the apartment was added a few years ago by the late Mr. Albert Gardiner."

"I had no idea there was so much land," Katherine said in surprise.

He smiled. "It is really a small remnant of what was once a tremendous estate, Mrs. Gardiner. In Beechwood there is a row of little apartments, which were originally the stables. In fact, the whole area of the town was once a part of the estate."

Katherine's eyes widened at the opulent image conjured up by his words. "I had no idea it was something like that. I don't think my ex-husband knew very much about it either."

"Probably not. The relationship is so distant and involved that we had considerable trouble tracing it."

"But it's the same family name isn't it?"

"Oh yes, but that was part of the trouble. Gardiner is a pretty common name. We had to go a long way back in the family history to find the right branch and then trace it back to the present again."

He seemed proud of the accomplishment. It occurred to

Katherine that Charles' casual disposal of his inheritance without even seeing it must have been disappointing.

"What happened to the rest of the estate and the family who owned it?"

"Well, the holdings just sort of melted away over the years. Several times it was divided among succeeding generations. The girls, naturally, took their portions into their husband's families. As in most families, there was a wastrel or two who sold or gambled away their shares.

"Finally there were about eighty acres left and two Gardiners, a young boy and a girl who were second cousins. Each had a claim on the land. They settled it by getting married."

"The perfect happy ending!" Katherine's laugh was sarcastic.

"Almost," Mr. Worthingham answered quietly. "They were deeply devoted to each other and they both loved that old house but unfortunately they never had the large family they so desperately wanted."

"No children in that huge place?"

"She had four pregnancies but only one child, Albert, survived past six months. I suppose it was only natural that they should have coddled and spoiled him, but the result was tragic. They gave him everything he wanted even though it meant selling most of their acreage to meet his demands. He was a mean spiteful child and a grasping self-centered man."

Katherine watched his face as he continued and she knew the Gardiners had been his friends as well as clients.

"He could be charming when he wanted to. He married three times, all wealthy women. When the money was gone or he couldn't get any more from his wife, the charm vanished. By then the ladies were only too happy to grant him his freedom. His first wife was

going to restore the mansion. She had the house wired for electricity
before they separated. The last one built that garage apartment for
him as the price of her freedom.

"After his father died years ago, he quarreled violently with
his mother because she refused to sell her home and give him what he
regarded as his rightful inheritance. He threatened to come back with
a truck and take all her priceless antique furniture and sell it. She said
he was bluffing, but after her death, I found the house as you saw it
last night."

A deep personal antipathy was apparent in the old lawyer's
voice. Katherine detected a rather grim relish as he added, "Fate
fooled him at the end, though. He never lived long enough after his
mother's death to complete the sale of the property."

Before she could ask what happened, Mrs. Bryson came in
and set a well-filled legal folder on the desk. Mrs. Gardiner's will was
lying on top of it. Mr. Worthingham picked up the document and
began skimming through it.

"Except for one bequest, this will is a simple transfer device.
Mrs. Gardiner left the property to her son. He died without making a
will. Charles Gardiner is the nearest living relative and he has
transferred his interest to you."

Katherine nodded and he continued.

"The codicil that affects you concerns the cash inheritance."

"I didn't know there was any money."

"It isn't a large amount and its use is legally limited. She left it
in trust for house improvements. It can't be used for anything else.
This codicil explains," and he began to read from the will:

"The above mentioned five thousand dollars represents
income from this property and is hereby set aside for the
improvement and repairs of said property. If not so used, the total

sum is to become the property of the Christian Children's Orphanage."

Katherine was intrigued. "That seems odd. I never heard of a house inheriting anything before."

He laughed. "I never heard it put just that way before. It isn't really so unusual for a sum of money to be legally set-aside for a specific purpose. I guess his mother just didn't want Albert to squander what little was left. The codicil is binding," he added. "The money must be used only for the house."

"I wouldn't dream of trying to cheat the house out of its inheritance," Katherine said emphatically. "I'd be afraid to."

The lawyer seemed startled at her words.

"What makes you say that?"

In her turn, Katherine was a little startled at his reaction.

"Why, nothing. I was just joking." She thought about it a moment. "I guess that's not entirely true. There's something about that house which intimidates me. It echoes! Probably, if it were full of furniture and people it would be different, but right now it's creepy!"

"Creepy how?" He was insistent. "Do you have any specific reason for saying that?"

There was something in his manner that reminded Katherine of Lily's attitude. Did he also think there was something to be afraid of in that house? Then she realized her remarks about the place must have made her appear a little childish. She told him, a bit sheepishly, about the chimney swifts.

He smiled. "Imagination can do some really terrifying things." As Lily had, he seemed relieved.

"Mr. Worthingham," there was no answering smile in her direct gaze, "that wasn't what you had in mind, was it? What is there to be afraid of in that house?"

"Absolutely nothing," he answered positively, "but when there has been a violent death in a house, the superstitious inevitably begin seeing ghosts."

"Ghosts! You mean the house is supposed to be haunted?"

"That's the idea," he said a little dryly, watching her closely, as if measuring the effect of his words.

Try as she might, Katherine couldn't deny a slight tingle of goose flesh along the back of her arms.

"What happened? Who was murdered?"

"The local people say Albert was killed by the ghost of his mother because he was going to sell the house she loved. Actually, it was a freak accident. The old plaster in that house is unusually thick and heavy and a large area broke loose from the ceiling in the middle of the night. A jagged piece pierced his temple killing him instantly."

"That's gruesome!" She shuddered. "I wondered about that hole in the ceiling, but I never would have thought of anything like that."

"You don't believe in ghosts?"

"I never have," she said soberly, "but in view of what my imagination did to me last night, I think I'd be more comfortable if I found someone to stay with me."

"Then you'll be staying in the house?"

"Of course, until I can sell it." She eyed him candidly. "I couldn't afford to keep it even if I wanted to, and besides it's too big for one person. It needs a family."

"You're right, of course," he said quietly, "but I am sorry to see it pass out of the family." With a resigned air he pulled some papers out of the folder and marked the places where she was to sign.

For the next hour the old lawyer led her through the contents of the folder. There were a number of papers, including several deeds.

The history was confusing because many of the Gardiners bore the same first names from one generation to the next. Some of the pages were yellowed with age and the ink was faded. A number of maps, many hand-drawn, showed the gradual shrinkage of the original holding. Katherine felt again the sense of living history that had surrounded her in the old house and signed the documents with a feeling of sadness at the ending of an era.

"Probate should take about six months," the lawyer informed her cheerfully. "That should give you time to get it in shape to sell. What do you plan to do?"

"I don't know, exactly," Katherine admitted. "What I was prepared to spend is a drop in the bucket to what that big old house needs. I guess I will just do some cleaning and a little painting. I don't suppose I can use that five thousand until it's through probate?"

"You're right, but I can recommend that the bank make you a personal loan against it. As long as it is spent on the house, the account secures it. Just be sure you keep records and receipts of all you spend, otherwise the estate will demand its money back."

He said it jokingly, but Katherine knew this was a real possibility. If she decided to accept his recommendation, she would have to be very careful to see that every cent went into the house and that she could prove it.

CHAPTER FOUR

When Katherine left the executor's office, she carried the folder of papers, the lawyer's promise to write a recommendation to a Beechwood bank and the address of a Beechwood realtor. She also carried many doubts about her survival in the pit her anger and pride had dug for her. For an instant, she even considered throwing in the towel and telling Charles he could have his white elephant back; she'd take her rightful share in alimony, but only for an instant. No way would she give him that satisfaction.

It was so obvious that Charles was trying to salve his guilty conscience with money. He wanted to pension me off, she thought, like a faithful old family servant. She could still hear her own angry words scornfully throwing his offer of generous alimony back at him.

"I gave up my career for you, Charles. I could have been a top professional decorator, but, no, you thought I should stay home and raise the children. Now the children are gone and you don't need your housekeeper anymore."

"Well, let me tell you this, Charles, I don't need you! I can still be a decorator. I still have my talent. I don't need anything from you. I can take care of myself."

The little old lady in her dream had said, "No looking back and no more tears." That's the way it's going to be, Katherine assured herself, but right now she couldn't quite see how she was going to do it.

The morning had made her so acutely conscious of her dowdy appearance that she refused an invitation to lunch with Mr. Worthingham. Now hunger added to her depressed mood and her stomach began to growl for attention. Near the off-ramp to Beechwood she spotted a hamburger stand with car service and pulled off the freeway. She rolled to a stop in the half-empty parking lot and leaned dejectedly against the cushions as she waited for service.

The food was good and her body responded with revived energy. Sipping her coffee, she gazed idly around, absently aware of a slight lifting of her spirits now that she had eaten.

It was obvious this had been a quiet residential area before the freeway exit arrived. Now a few small businesses had been inserted among the modest homes. It was still a pretty street with lawns and trees sweltering a bit in the heat, which had followed the rain. A LANGHEN REALTY shingle on the opposite corner caught her attention. She recognized it as the firm recommended by Mr. Worthingham. Without a definite plan for the next step in handling her problems, Katherine decided she might benefit from talking to the realtor. Re-parking her car out of the way at the edge of the fast food lot, she walked across the street.

Formerly a small home, the business now looked on the neighborhood through plate-glass office windows, but a tiny lawn and a front porch gave it an informal air. Inside, the blend of home and business resulted in an inviting den-like effect. There were two overstuffed leather chairs and a huge carved walnut desk flanked by a bank of file cabinets. A tall man arose from his work at the desk when she entered, placing his pipe aside as he greeted her.

"Good afternoon. May I help you?"

He appeared to be about her own age, casually dressed, a

moderate tan emphasizing silver-gray temples. He was ruggedly handsome, with a smile that was pure sex appeal.

For the second time that day she became aware of her frumpy appearance. She fumbled for words to introduce her errand. Not since adolescence, had Katherine felt so painfully aware of her shortcomings. She wished she had chosen another day to stop here.

Diplomatically ignoring her discomfort, he came to the rescue.

"Oh, yes, Mrs. Gardiner. I'm Paul Langhen," he said, extending his hand. "Mr. Worthingham informed me of your arrival. I was handling the sale of the property for the former owner when he died. If you would like, I would be happy to act in the same capacity for you."

"I really don't know exactly what I'm going to do," she said uncertainly. "I thought perhaps you could help me decide."

He looked surprised. "Have a seat," he motioned to one of the big leather chairs, "and we'll talk about it."

He returned to his desk and placed a scratch pad and some pencils in front of him.

"Do I understand that you wish to keep this property?"

" Oh no. I intend to sell it but I don't know if I should try to fix it up. I have very little money compared to what that place needs. Mr. Worthingham says I can borrow against the five thousand that was left for the house, but I'm afraid that what I could do might not raise the price enough to return the five thousand."

"What would you like to do if you could?"

"Oh!" Her eyes glowed. "What I wouldn't like to do! It's such a grand old house. It's really a piece of our historical past. It must have been beautiful and Mr. Worthingham said it had been totally self-supporting. They made or grew nearly everything they needed. Places like that just don't exist in this century. It seems a shame that the only thing left of an estate like that is the house. I'd love to be able to completely restore it, but that would cost thousands and a lot of money is just what I don't have at present. If you and Mr. Worthingham think it will pay, I'll do what I can with the money available and try to get the best price possible."

He gave her a warm smile that made her feel he was taking a special interest. Picking up a pencil he said, "Let's see if we can figure out just how much you can do with what you have to work with. First, I think you are going to have to install some sort of modern heating system. Those fireplaces would never be acceptable today."

" Mr. Langhen," she said firmly, "that would require too much money. I'll be lucky if I can manage paint and new wallpaper."

"Now just wait a minute. First; my name is Paul," he smiled. "Second; let me show you something."

He pulled a slightly tattered Sears catalog from a desk drawer and hunted through it until he found the furnace section. He drew a circle around a picture with a price under it and shoved the book over to her.

"See, he said triumphantly, "the biggest unit would take about half of that five thousand and you will have quite a bit left over for paint and paper." Later she would remember that she hadn't looked at the date on that catalog.

"That's a lot less than I would have estimated," she admitted.

Having this first step within her financial reach made the project look more encouraging.

"I took interior decorating in college," she informed him. "Doing the work myself will cut labor expense and there will be that much more for materials."

She didn't think it was necessary to admit that she didn't get her degree because she dropped out to get married.

"I assumed you would," he said approvingly as his eyes met hers with an odd unsettling effect that made her pulse beat a little faster, "but it might be wise to hire an assistant. I'm sure the profit from a successful sale would justify such an expense."

Although Katherine knew an interest in his client's problems was a necessary part of Paul Langhen's profession, she felt his interest was gradually becoming more personal as they talked. With this encouragement and the outline on his scratch pad, she began to have hope that her situation might not be so bad, after all.

Paul also brushed aside any concerns about the money she would need. He assured her that any bank would regard the property as good security for a loan.

"The recommendations of your lawyer and your real estate agent will practically open the bank vault for you," he joked.

For a moment Katherine wondered what he meant by that. She had no intention of borrowing any more than the five thousand that she felt legitimately belonged to the house. Then she decided that must be what he was talking about.

Katherine savored the words 'your lawyer, your real estate agent' It was remarkable how much more secure the world became with the acquisition of a staff of competent advisors. For the first time since she had explored that enormous dark house, she began to feel a bit optimistic again. Paul talked to her as if they had formed a partnership. He seemed to take her professional ability for granted which was balm to Katherine's ego. At one time the burning enthusiasm for her chosen work filled her thoughts to the exclusion of everything else, but her marriage had replaced that spark for a long time. Now colors and spatial relationships began to come back in the struggle to resurrect lines of thought that had been buried since her college years. Her brain felt rusty, but stimulated. It was exciting, and so was the man across the desk.

Laughing at a quip, Katherine was shocked to realize she was responding to Paul with very girlish emotions. She felt foolish at the realization and tried to concentrate on what he was saying. So far he had treated her with the correct courtesy that is usually reserved for an elderly Aunt. With wry inner amusement, she could picture his careful footwork if he guessed his charm was eliciting a romantic response from a frumpy older woman. Such a handsome self-assured man would surely have been pursued by many women. He was certain to be a skilled diplomat where the other sex was concerned.

With the conviction that the reactions of a teenager indicated approaching senility in a woman her age, she concentrated her attention on the solutions to her financial problems.

Although Katherine ended the interview realistically aware that Paul's interest in her affairs was rooted in business, she made no attempt to deny her pleasure in his company. He was a very attractive man and it had been a long time since she had looked at a member of the opposite sex through eyes of freedom. She was facing a whole new world and it was enough to adapt to each experience as it came.

CHAPTER FIVE

Katherine opened her eyes with a lingering feeling that something good had happened. For a moment her mind dwelt pleasurably on Paul Langhen's smiling face, but there was something else teasing her memory. Then her eyes rested on the rocking chair and she remembered. She had awakened in the night to see the little old lady with the cane sitting there. She didn't speak, just sat and rocked in front of the fire in silence. It was the comfortable silence of companionship and Katherine went back to sleep knowing she was welcome in this house. It was all a dream, of course, but the pleasure was still there to send her spirits soaring with the morning sun.

The air was chilly enough to make a fire desirable, but the dampness seemed to be nearly gone. Again the sensation crossed her mind that the house was arousing from a dormant state, beginning to be alive once more. The inability to control such flights of imagination annoyed her, but only momentarily. She felt too good this morning and there was too much to do to dwell on any serious doubts about her mental stability.

The first thing she wanted to do was call at the Beechwood Bank. In spite of her new staff of advisers, the idea of being able to walk in and borrow five thousand dollars on her tenuous form of security seemed incredible. She would not actually believe it until the money was in hand.

Then, if the financial part worked out all right, the next step was to find an extra pair of hands to help with the work ahead of her. Lily had suggested a girl from a farm several miles down the road might be available. I might ask her to stay nights, too, Katherine thought, but she hadn't mentioned it because it seemed too much like an admission of cowardice.

Lily arrived just as she finished breakfast.

"I thought you could show me the house first," Katherine told her. 'Then I'll have some idea of what I'm going to have to do."

"I only went through the whole house once, myself," Lily said. "I guess it was a beautiful place a long time ago, but it's sure an awful mess now."

Together they toured the lower floor. In addition to the part she had already seen, Lily showed her how the panels of the wall between the family room and the parlor could be folded back to each side, making one tremendous room. For an instant, Katherine's imagination filled the immense space with a scene of old-fashioned waltzing couples whirling about a glittering ballroom. Then she sighed. That was part of the past for this house. Not many people live like that anymore.

She tried to form some idea of the best way to use the house's money if she got it.

The whole house was built on such a grand scale that Katherine decided any room in the place could surrender the amount of floor space needed for the bathroom she was determined to install. The trouble was she couldn't decide where one should go, or where the money was going to come from to build it.

"This place is too big for me," Lily volunteered as they headed back to the kitchen. "Nobody needs a house this big unless he's a governor or a senator or a bigwig of some kind."

"Well," Katherine laughed, "maybe I'll just have to find one of those bigwigs to sell it to."

"That won't be easy, Mrs. Gardiner," Lily said soberly. "There's only one part of the whole house that I really like and it's too small to live in."

"I'm surprised there's anything small in this house. Where on earth is it?"

Lily showed her an almost hidden door under the back stairs that led to a little round room next to the added-on bathroom. An electric water heater stood in the center of the space that had once formed the base supporting a water tower. It was like a windowless round closet with dust and cobwebs coating the white tank, the light bulb and the electric cord suspending it from the ceiling. Katherine stopped in disbelief just inside the door.

"You like this place?"

"Oh, no," Lily corrected her, "the room upstairs."

Trying to hold her breath against the dust Katherine climbed the narrow circular stairway around the wall to the small room above. At the top of the stair, she involuntarily paused in the doorway and drew a quick breath. The room was only about nine feet across, but four tall narrow bay windows made the area appear much larger. It was so bright that dust and cobwebs hardly registered against the view of blue sky and tops of distant trees. With built-in window seats, the shallow bays framed views of the countryside in all directions. In the rest of the house the woodwork was dark and heavy looking, up here it had once been white. Faded roses still showed in the wallpaper.

Katherine was charmed by the remnants of beauty clinging to this little hideaway. She could picture herself sewing or reading in its privacy, or just watching distant columns of chimney smoke rising above the woods. For an instant she was a little sorry to think of preparing the house for someone else to live in.

"You're right Lily. This is a special room. It's so cozy and the view is wonderful."

"That's what I thought," the housekeeper said with satisfaction.

The last stop on the morning's tour was the root cellar. Lily collected a couple of flashlights and led the way outside to a slanted plank door on the ground. She lifted it with a great deal of effort to expose rock steps leading down under the house. With a slight shudder Katherine followed their flashlight beams down into the musty dark. The circles of light picked out rough rock walls constructed without mortar. The small excavation was divided into two rooms, one lined with shelves containing a few empty jars. The other one was bare except for a coal chute protruding from the wall. Every surface was liberally coated with coal dust.

"I suppose coal made a hotter fire in those little fireplaces," Katherine observed, flinching away from a web across her cheek.

Lily started to answer but sneezed from the dust. Like a cave, the cellar had an earthy smell and spiders everywhere. Katherine didn't linger and emerged brushing vigorously at her hair to rid it of clinging strands of sticky web. It was a relief to be out in the sun again.

The morning was well along and she hurried to get ready to visit the bank. With yesterday's experience in mind, she eyed a row of out of style dresses with distaste. Finally she selected a pantsuit, mostly because it fit without stretching the seams.

All the way to the local shopping district, she was hopeful one minute and pessimistic the next. Even if the bank advanced the whole amount, it would hardly make a dent in what that house really needed.

Paint and paper were absolutely necessary. A modern furnace would take at least half the money. She didn't know what a new bathroom would cost, but it was bound to be expensive and she simply didn't have that much money. In a moment of depression, she thought maybe it would be smarter to give up now and go back to California and try to find a job.

Again she rejected that course. No matter what lay ahead, self-respect demanded an effort. She resolved to be her most persuasive in the interview ahead. Everything depended on this first step.

In the end, the whole business turned out to be ridiculously easy. It wasn't even necessary to ask for a loan. The bank president, Mr. Minyard, came out of his office as soon as she gave her name to a teller.

"I've been expecting you," he smiled. "Mr. Worthingham called about finding the heir to the Gardiner property. He gave you quite a recommendation. In addition, your background in interior decoration offers considerable security for making this type of personal loan."

Katherine was startled. That last bit of information could only have come from Paul and it made her feel a little deceptive. She hoped the banker never found out how shallow that background really was. The VIP treatment was both gratifying and frightening. Now she was really committed.

In a short time, Katherine was back out on the street with a new account at the bank and a checkbook in her bag.

Typically, the lady's first thought was for the proper clothing. Nothing in her closet was appropriate for launching a battle against spiders and peeling wallpaper. She began walking along the street, searching in store windows for something suitable. Several small shops offered women's clothing, but they all seemed to cater to teenagers in both style and size. In the third block, however, there was a department store with a section labeled 'The Big Girl Shop'. Here she found blue jeans and shirts that would fit.

While she occasionally wore a pantsuit, Katherine's wardrobe was mostly housedresses or summer shorts. The stiff blue denim felt strange and rough against her skin.

I look enormous, Katherine thought viewing her reflection in the mirror, but they're practical. She bought two checked shirts, one red, one blue, and two pairs of the jeans. After adding a pair of sturdy oxfords and a half dozen pairs of socks, she felt adequately prepared for hard labor.

She drove home in mounting eagerness and excitement. The easy success of her first move seemed to make the whole venture less formidable. Even the bank was betting on her, she thought. The next step was that farm girl to help with the work.

CHAPTER SIX

Lily was waiting on the porch steps. Since Katherine had forgotten lunch, she gulped a glass of milk and a cold hard-boiled egg without sitting down. At the moment food was unimportant.

In the car, Lily told her to turn left out of the driveway.

"Okay. How far is it?"

"About five miles." Lily was silent for a moment, then asked hopefully, "Are you going to stay on here, Mrs. Gardiner?"

"Only long enough to put the house in shape to sell," Katherine answered.

"Oh," Lily said in a disappointed tone.

"Why," Katherine asked, although she had already guessed.

"It's just that we like it so much here," Lily admitted. "We hoped it would be a permanent job."

"Well," Katherine offered comfortingly, "perhaps whoever buys it will need you to stay on. It's just too big a house for me alone. At any rate, it will be at least six months before we can get it on the market. I hope you can stay with me until then."

"Of course," Lily assured her. "We'll stay as long as you need us."

Noting that Lily really did not seem surprised, the heiress ruefully concluded that both her marital and financial status had already been the subject of local gossip. It is amazing how such news travels through a neighborhood.

After passing several small country homes, Lily indicated a gray, weathered two-story house on the right side of the road. Shadows of paint under the eaves showed it had once been yellow. A number of bricks had fallen from one corner of the chimney. Tall weeds almost hid a vast assortment of junk, including two battered old cars. On one side of the yard there was a long-handled pump mounted on a cement block. At first glance, it appeared to be just another piece of junk, but a footpath through the weeds indicated that the well provided the water for the house.

Katherine pulled off the road and stopped in front of a leaning fence that gaped with broken or missing pickets. She looked at Lily a little questioningly.

"This is the right place," Lily assured her. "I brought her home one day when she had a flat tire on her bike."

Wondering how anything but sloth could come from such neglected surroundings, Katherine asked, "Do you know if she is a good worker?"

The other woman nodded. "She does house work for several ladies in town and they say she is a hard worker and very dependable."

"Well, we'll see." Katherine was dubious.

Lily led the way, Katherine following a little reluctantly, her eyes on the dirt path.

Suddenly, with a heart-stopping roar, a huge dog lunged at them out of the weeds. They both froze, eyes wide, breath caught in their throats. The threat was cut short by a chain that jerked taut as he reached its limit. Snarling, he fought against the heavy choke collar until a short, fat woman with dyed red hair opened the screen door and shouted, "Shep! Shut up!"

As she watched the animal sullenly trail back along his chain, Katherine was aware of very shaky knees. Lily pulled a handkerchief from her pocket with trembling fingers and rubbed moist palms.

The woman on the porch said, "I hope Shep didn't scare you ladies. He's mostly bluff."

Her eyebrows were narrow black crescents that gave her an inquiring look and she had eaten most of her smeared lipstick. Katherine could have sworn there was a smirk of amusement lingering in the chubby face.

"Well, he certainly convinced us he meant it," Katherine said trying to subdue a feeling of righteous resentment.

"What can I do for you ladies?" the woman asked.

"Mrs. Gardiner needs a hired girl," Lily announced. "She came to talk to you about getting Dorothea to help her."

"Oh, glad to meet'cha, Miz Gardiner. I'm Liz Jenkins. Dorothea's not home yet, but she'll be along pretty soon. C'mon in an' sit a spell till she comes."

Although her words did not exclude Lily, her manner did. Katherine wasn't sure whether this indicated prejudice or just slovenly manners. Lily, with a lifetime of experience to guide her, recognized veiled bigotry and tactfully sidestepped the situation.

"I'll run up to the next farm and get us some fresh butter and eggs while you wait, Mrs. Gardiner," she said quickly.

Katherine didn't want to stay, but Lily was gone before she could object. Mrs. Jenkins ushered her guest into a dingy, cluttered room. Flinging scattered clothing into a pile at one end of a couch, her hostess urged her to sit in the cleared space. Katherine did so gingerly, reluctant to come in contact with the grimy cushions.

"Would you like some coffee, Miz Gardiner? It'll only take a minute to heat up the pot."

Greasy soiled spots darkening the material stretched over the ample bust and stomach of the other woman drew Katherine's eye as she hastily declined. Aware that she was staring, she looked away and wondered if Mrs. Jenkins ever bathed or washed her clothes. She was relieved when the lady decided not to sit next to her on the couch.

Lighting a cigarette, the Jenkins woman leaned back in a rocking chair and pushed her thick bushy hair back with an affected air. Coquettish gestures seemed out of character with such grossness.

"Dorry's not my real daughter, you know," she confided. "She's my stepdaughter. I'd had'da been ten years old to have a girl her age now. A' course I was real young when I got married," she laughed, "but not that young."

Katherine didn't know how old the girl was, but she was sure this woman was older than she implied. She didn't know what to say, but soon realized she wasn't expected to reply, just listen.

Liz Jenkins appeared to regard this visit as a social call and her social conversation consisted of a detailed recital of her personal life.

"My first husbin was a real handsome devil, but he turned out to be as mean as he was good lookin'. Nearly every payday he'd come home drunk and spoilin fer a fight so one payday, I just waited 'til he passed out and took what was left of his paycheck and grabbed the first bus I saw. Turned out it was goin' to Baltimore. I always wanted to live in a big city, so I jus' hopped off right in front of a hamburger joint an' went in and got a burger 'cause I never had nothin' to eat all day."

Momentarily Katherine wondered where Liz had come from, but there was no chance to ask. The story went on.

"That fry cook fell for me as soon as I walked in the door an' he wouldn't let me pay for the burger an' gave me a job waitin' tables. He had a room upstairs, but there was only one bed so I had'da sleep with him, but he was real nice.

Then one night Bruce came in. He was just the best lookin' thing I ever saw, and did he ever fall for me! I told him I wasn't divorced yet, but he said he wasn't gonna let no little piece of paper stand in the way of our love, so I moved in with him."

Her voice droned on from one tedious affair to another, each emphasizing Liz's fatal attraction. Katherine's attention wandered until mention of Dorothea's father reminded her why she was here.

"He was the handsomest thing you ever saw an' he sure was crazy about me. His wife's family sure treated him dirty. When his wife was killed in a car wreck, they kicked him out; said he was drunk when it happened. Course the real reason was they just didn't think he was good enough for their high society family. They tried to take Dorothea away from him too, but the judge said her Daddy had first rights to his own daughter. Poor man was so broke up over losing his wife he started drinkin' pretty heavy. He was sick a lot an' I took good care of him an' his girl, too."

Liz Jenkins apparently saw nothing contradictory about the fact that it was his drinking that led to his wife's death.

"He used to call Dorry his little goldmine, cause he said she was supposed to come into money when she turned twenty-one and we'd be on easy street for the rest of our lives. An' then he went an' died. An' you know what? He was liein' 'bout that money. She didn't inherit nothin'. All I got for all those years was his kid to raise."

Katherine was dismayed to think of what life must have been for the child in these squalid surroundings. At least, she thought, the woman cared enough to give the girl a home. A few more words, however, disclosed the real reason behind her action.

"A'course we're poor as church mice an' me bein' in poor

health, I can't work no more, an' welfare don't pay very much. It's only right that the girl should pay me back for all I done for her. She owes me."

Disgust competing with boredom, Katherine was heartily wishing for Lily's return, when a stringy-haired youngster came in, banging the door behind her.

"Maw, I'm home."

The sight of a stranger in the room halted her in shy silence. She was about ten and a little cleaner than her mother, but not by much.

"This is Mrs. Gardiner, Dearie," her mother said in honeyed tones.

The girl's only response was a wide-eyed stare until the falsely sweet voice prodded, "Say 'Hello', Virginia, and then go tend to your little brother."

With a wary eye on her mother, Virginia bobbed her head, "How'do, Ma'am." She tossed her schoolbooks onto a cluttered chair and crossed the room to push aside a faded calico drape. Behind it was an alcove just large enough for a baby's crib. The child, a little less than a year old, lay outstretched on his back sound asleep. Katherine looked at him and almost gagged.

Before he went to sleep, he had been given a fresh peach. Mashed pieces of fruit stained gray sheets and clung to the crib bars. He wore only a diaper, and much of his exposed skin was coated in grimy peach juice. Flies buzzed over a bottle half-full of soured milk. One crawled across a sticky little cheek to the corner of the baby's open mouth. An involuntary twitch sent the fly darting off and the child whimpered.

A strong smell of urine filled the room as his sister removed plastic pants to change his diaper. He cried out in his sleep when the air reached raw red buttocks. Virginia spread the wet diaper on a line strung behind the cast iron stove and removed one that had already dried there. Ignoring both stains and pungent odor, she folded it into the required shape. Katherine winced as the girl pinned it around the raw skin and tugged the plastic panties up without awakening the infant.

Her stomach turning, Katherine wondered that the tot had survived its first summer in such surroundings. One thing she had definitely decided, she didn't want to hire anyone from this family. First, patching up that big house was going to be real physical labor, and it was clear hard work was not part of the Jenkin's philosophy. Second, close daily association with anyone with such filthy personal habits would be repellent, to say the least. Surely, there must be other help available; people a little better acquainted with soap and water.

Mounting impatience to be out of this place turned to anger with Lily for being gone so long. Only half hearing the other woman's endless monologue, Katherine listened hopefully for every car to stop, but it was a bicycle that finally stemmed the flow. Mrs. Jenkins paused at the sound of a bike being pushed up on the porch to a resting place against the wall. She waved at the door with her cigarette.

"That's Dorry, now."

Trapped! Now how was she to get out of hiring the girl without making an enemy? She recognized the sound of her car stopping out in front. Lily was finally back, too late.

The door opened and so did Katherine's eyes in surprise. She had been expecting a teenager, but this was a young woman. In no way did she appear to belong to this dismal household. It wasn't just that she was exceptionally pretty, but she was so clean, from faded blue jeans to shiny gold hair. Her fair skin was lightly tanned and exercise had raised warm flags of color in her cheeks. As the younger child had, she stopped and looked questioningly from her stepmother to Katherine.

"This is Mrs. Gardiner, Dorry, the one that inherited that big old house up the road. She wants you should work for her."

The blue eyes searched Katherine's face eagerly.

"How do you do? What kind of work is it, Mrs. Gardiner, house cleaning?"

"Never mind what kind, Miss Goody-two-shoes. You'll do whatever you're told to do." Plainly, Mrs. Jenkins enjoyed being a bully.

"Sure, Maw," Dorothea answered patiently. "I was just asking."

Katherine's dislike of the woman quickly turned to antagonism. She was surprised to feel a strong desire to protect the young woman from her.

"It will be pretty hard work, Dorothea, cleaning and painting, getting the house ready to sell."

"What was you aimin' to pay?" Mrs. Jenkins asked.

Katherine hesitated. If she was right, her financial situation was already common gossip in the neighborhood. The woman couldn't hope for any big amount of money, but it would have to be enough to justify eliminating the girl's present contribution.

"Well," she explained slowly, "I don't have much money right now. I thought, maybe, Dorothea would be willing to work for room and board right now. Then I could pay her wages in a lump sum when I sell the house."

"That'd be all right with me, Maw," the girl said quietly.

The woman flashed her an angry glance.

"You're in a mighty big hurry to leave your home, Dearie!

Suppose she can't sell the house, or something?"

It was plain to Katherine that 'or something' translated into a fear of losing the 'bird in hand' for a possibly elusive one in the bush. With only the faintest edge of irony, she offered to draw up a contract guaranteeing Dorothea's wages, and recklessly tossed in a bonus for the delay.

Avarice rose to the bait. A large lump sum was obviously an enticing glimpse of wealth. Although not entirely satisfied, Mrs. Jenkins agreed to the arrangement, with the implicit understanding that all income belonged to the loving stepmother. Dorothea was allowed no say in the matter. It was necessary to bargain in this house, Katherine conceded to herself, but payment would be made in her house, and to the employee, not her self-appointed stepmother. Katherine would have liked to take the girl home right then, but Mrs. Jenkins' shrewd eye had detected the instant empathy between them. She was already on the defensive. Such a suggestion might cause complications if the woman saw it as a threat to her continued domination. As indifferently as possible, Katherine made arrangements to deliver a wage contract and pick up her new employee the next day.

Dorothea appeared to be over twenty-one Katherine thought, and wondered why she submitted to that bullying manner. Liz Jenkins had no valid legal standing according to her own story. The contract would be worthless, but the Gardiner conscience never even twitched. It was exactly what that unscrupulous woman deserved.

Lily was waiting patiently in the passenger seat when Katherine went out to the car. Neither of them said a word until the car was turned around and headed for home. Katherine took a deep breath of fresh air.

"Have you ever been in that house?"

"No, I just drove the girl home one day."

"But, you knew what it was like?"

"I had heard some neighborhood gossip about it, that's all."

"You left me there on purpose!" Her voice rose a bit with annoyance. "Why, Lily? Did you think it was funny?"

"Oh, no, Mrs. Gardiner!" Lily's hand flew to her dark cheek as if she had been struck. "I'd never do that anything like that. It was just that she didn't want to ask me in her house and I wanted you to see what it was like. I thought maybe you could do something."

"Do something?" Comprehension dawned. "About Dorothea?"

Lily nodded. "She's such a nice person and that mean lazy woman has convinced her it is her duty to support the family. I think she'd leave Mrs. Jenkins in a minute, but she worries about the children.

A cat's-paw! Lily had conned her! For a second Katherine was indignant at being used, then grudgingly impressed. Lily had certainly gauged her reactions correctly. Finally, all the strains of the past several hours were released in a shout of laughter. She pressed Lily's hand in amnesty, explaining between pleased chuckles, that she had indeed, done something. Her companion's relish and admiration added spice to the telling and they arrived home on a note of elation at having scored a coup, however unintentional it may have been on Katherine's part

Knowing Fred would be waiting for his evening meal, Katherine sent Lily home. Cooking for herself alone seemed a waste of time. She heated a can of vegetable soup and ate it absentmindedly, her thoughts occupied with drawing up a contract. Afterward, she opened the typewriter and began her composition.

Several hours and many sheets of paper later, an acceptable

result emerged. Looking it over, she decided it contained enough legalese to confuse anybody. There were two copies and Mrs. Jenkins would be required to sign each one along with Dorothea. Katherine added her signature and put the documents away, feeling both self-satisfied and a little guilty. It was almost like a confidence game because she didn't intend that Mrs. Jenkins should benefit by one penny.

This final act brought an overwhelming awareness of fatigue. Early or not, it was her bedtime. Blurrily, before sleep closed her mind, the whole fantastic day passed in drowsy review. So many things; so many emotions crowded in between sunrise and sunset. It seemed that some of it must have happened yesterday.

There was a rustling in the chimney; no fires today, so the swifts were back. Odd, how different the sound this time. She liked hearing it. Everything about the house was different, somehow, not so empty or depressing. On the edge of surrendering to gentle darkness, she was faintly aware that Lily must have left her window open. The last thing she heard was the hypnotic seesaw of wooden rockers on the floor in front of the fireplace.

CHAPTER SEVEN

The muscles in her back felt stiff as Katherine straightened up from pulling weeds along the driveway. Absently she rubbed her back and looked around at the bright fall foliage signaling the end of summer. Everything seemed so different than it had when she first saw the place. It wasn't just the change taking place in the house, but a growing confidence in her own ability.

At first she had thrown herself almost desperately into the job, overwhelmed by the size of the undertaking. Without direction or plan, she worked compulsively, steaming brittle old wallpaper, scraping mold and plastering bare places; pushing herself to trembling exhaustion. At night she was too tired to eat and unable to stay awake at the table. Often she was only half aware of being aided to undress. Sometimes she was not even sure whether it was Lily or Dorothea urging her through the motions. The only clear memory of those first weeks was of the aching weariness that seemed to penetrate her bones.

Then her soft body began to harden. Flabby muscles became more elastic, and her appetite came back. Although they shrank in washing, the blue jeans seemed to fit more loosely every day. As the numbing fatigue passed, so did the frenzied waste of energy. She began to plan her work instead of simply attacking without design and learned to use and direct the efforts of her helpers.

Lily did the cooking, washing and small amount of housekeeping demanded by their disorganized existence. Fred was a part time fireman on the railroad, but on his days at home he cut wood for the stove and helped with some of the heavier work. He also cut wood for the little fireplaces, although the summer heat turned Katherine's thoughts more in the direction of some way to cool the house.

Dorothea did whatever she was assigned, happily willing and apparently tireless. Only one thing she refused to do; to go upstairs alone after dark. In the daytime she would go up to sandpaper woodwork or steam and scrape wallpaper, but anything forgotten stayed there until morning. The dilapidated couch downstairs was her chosen bed.

There was no doubt; either, that Lily's views coincided with Dorothea's. All her housekeeping chores were finished by dusk or postponed until the next day. She simply would not stay in the big house after dark. In the first weeks Katherine was too tired to notice their behavior. Later, remembering her own fears, she was amused, but sympathetic. She supposed both her assistants would get over it eventually.

As she gazed, she felt a cool breeze, but the fall sun was still extremely warm on the back of her head and shoulders. Beads of perspiration trickled from her damp hairline. She wiped them away with a dusty shirtsleeve leaving dirt smudges just above her eyebrows. Some trees in her view were already stripped of their leaves, but others still carried brilliant daubs of color. Everywhere there were carpets of brown and gold leaves and a smell of wood smoke hung in the air. It was a beautiful autumn scene.

When she looked at the huge pile of weeds in front of her, she wondered how Charles would react if he knew what she was doing here.

You might find life less boring," he had once suggested, "if you would take up a hobby. Gardening is good exercise."

"That's a man's work," she had answered tartly. "I'm getting too old for hard labor, Charles."

"Well, maybe it would be too much for you," he had conceded sarcastically.

He'd be surprised, she thought, but not as surprised as she was.

Deciding there really wasn't time for idle admiration of the scenery, Katherine reluctantly turned from the view to gather an armload of the weeds at her feet. As she added them to the sizable mountain of rubbish developing beside the driveway, a car turned in from the road. It stopped momentarily where Dorothea was chopping away the dead canes in a clump of rose bushes, then continued as the girl pointed in Katherine's direction.

Katherine was vividly aware of a glow of pleasure when Paul Langhen stepped out of the driver's side and smiled at her over the top of the car. Removing the pipe from his mouth, he surveyed her closely. His eyebrows lifted a bit and the smile became a frankly approving grin.

"You've cut your hair. It looks good."

Katherine was absurdly pleased. "Had to. Couldn't keep it out of my face."

He came around the car and up the grassy bank of the driveway without taking his eyes from her. The steady gaze made her self-conscious. She knew he was really seeing her for the first time. Her flustered manner made him realize he was staring and brought back his usual casual bearing. So skilled was he in striking just the right note that she was at ease again almost immediately. She recognized his total control of the situation with mixed emotions. While it gave pleasure, it was also disconcerting to be handled so easily.

Paul turned as Dorothea came up the driveway with another load of cuttings for the trash pile. "I see girls are wearing a new style of make-up these days," he grinned.

Aware of a smear of mud on her cheek, she laughed and rubbed part of it off.

"I'm not the only one," she said looking at the dirt marks across Katherine's forehead.

"Let's go wash our faces," Katherine laughed. "It's time to quit work anyway. Will you stay for supper?" she asked Paul as they entered the kitchen.

"With pleasure," he said. "Hello, Lily. How's the best cook in the county this evening?"

Smiling, she looked up from the potatoes she was peeling.

"Thank you, Mr. Langhen. It's nice to see you again, but I'm not going to buy a house so you can just quit flattering me."

Katherine noticed, however, that she seemed willing to stay a little later than usual to make a special effort for their guest.

While the meal was being prepared, he toured the house offering complementary remarks about the work as they went from room to room. He seemed genuinely impressed. Katherine felt flattered that her efforts found approval in the eyes of a real estate professional.

In one of their frequent phone conversations, Katherine had asked, "Can't we keep the fireplaces someway, Paul?"

"They're really very impractical, Mrs. Gardiner. In this climate it takes central heating to keep such a large house comfortable."

"I know," she persisted, "but couldn't we have both? Those fireplaces give the house so much of its character."

"That's true," he agreed. "I'll send some diagrams of the fireplaces and the chimneys to
the furnace people and see if we can work something out."

"They need to know a lot of information about how the house is built, though, before they can submit a bid. I'll send them the sketches of the fireplaces and tell them what I know about the house and if it looks feasible, they'll send one of their experts out to prepare the bid."

It was a quiet evening with conversation centering on plans for the house, but Paul seemed in no hurry to leave. After the moment of his obvious surprise at the change in her appearance, he had dropped 'Katherine' and assumed 'Katy' on a more informal note. Every now and then she encountered an appraising glance that conveyed a warmer personal response. One such moment came when she showed him the nearly finished repair job in the ceiling of the Master bedroom.

"I'm going to move in here as soon as this is finished." He caught the rather appalled look on Dorothea's face, as well as the elaborate casualness in Katherine's voice, and grinned provokingly.

"That's a very good idea," was all he said, but the way he said it was almost a dare.

"Yes, I thought so," she answered loftily.

The grin widened, but he dropped the subject.

When they were straightening up the kitchen later, Dorothea brought it up again a little hesitantly.

"Are you really going to sleep in that room up there?"

"Of course, I am. I keep telling you there's nothing to be afraid of upstairs."

"But, that man, that other Mr. Gardiner, he was murdered in that room!"

"Dorothea! He was not murdered. It was just an accident that old plaster happened to collapse right over where he was sleeping."

"But, they say . . . "

"Who are they?"

"Everyone who lives around here. They all say his mother didn't want him to sell the house out of the Gardiner family, and he was going to do it anyway."

"And I'm going to do the same thing, is that it?" There was an edge of sarcasm to Katherine's voice.

"Well, you are," the girl said defensively.

"That is superstitious nonsense, and you know it!" Katherine was almost angry, partly because, against all common sense, that very thought had crossed her mind.

"Maybe it is nonsense like you say," Dorothea was near tears in her earnestness, "but there's an awful lot of people around here think different."

It's strange Katherine thought, sometimes Dorry's worldliness makes her appear to be a much older woman. Other times she seems to be defenselessly young.

"I know, I know, she said soothingly, but they're wrong, Dorry. Look, suppose they were right, they're not, but just suppose, don't you think an evil spirit could get me down here, just as easily as upstairs?"

Dorothea looked at her dubiously. Apparently this was a new thought.

"I suppose so."

"Then it doesn't make any difference where I sleep, does it?"

That drew a very unwilling, "I guess not."

"Well," Katherine closed the subject cheerfully, "there's no point in crossing our bridges tonight, anyway. There's a lot of work to be done before anyone can move upstairs."

Dorothea didn't say anything more, but she didn't seem particularly reassured, either. They finished the dishes in thoughtful silence.

The first thing Katherine did on gaining the privacy of her bedroom, was consult the mirror. She hadn't given it much thought lately. Now her ego demanded to see what had attracted Paul's attention.

What she saw was a woman who looked fifteen years younger than the one who had been reflected there when she first arrived. Cutting her hair short had encouraged its natural curl and the touch of silver made frosted highlights. A very light golden tan had heightened her color to a youthful glow. There was no scale in the house so she couldn't tell how much weight she had lost, but her blue jeans were so big that only a belt from one of her dresses kept her in them.

Realizing that she had not worn a dress since she came here, Katherine pulled several from the wardrobe and tried them on. They were too big. More than that, they no longer seemed to belong to her. The style was too severe, even drab. She was really not the same person anymore. It was more than just cutting her hair and losing a few pounds. The gray in her hair, the crinkles around her eyes were still there, but she seemed younger somehow, more vital.

Charles came to mind suddenly; a Charles plainly miserable with guilt and shame, yet at the same time, feverishly excited, as he tried to explain.

"I know it's a rotten thing to do, Katy. It's cruel and selfish, but I can't help it! She makes me feel so young! It's a new chance at life and I've got to take it now! There's so little time left. You can have anything you want, everything! Just let me go!"

With her new awareness she felt it was somehow easier to comprehend what had happened to him. It was a last chance to turn the clock back. The years had been passing inexorably, taking his youth with them, when this incredible miracle rekindled the dying fires. It was his assurance that age had not yet caught up with him, no matter what the calendar said. Even though Katherine told herself she understood, the sense of betrayal still burned.

Thinking of Charles opened the gates to memories. In her mind's eye, he appeared behind her in the mirror as he had the night before their 17th anniversary. She thought he had forgotten the date because he hadn't mentioned it.

"I shouldn't give you this until tomorrow," he said, "but I can't wait."

Katherine opened the tiny box to find a glittering green emerald pendant glowing in its cotton nest.

"Oh, Charles!"

Her eyes sparkled with tears. For most of her life she had dreamed of owning an emerald. It was her birthstone and Charles had promised she'd have one someday. But there was always the electric bill, or the water bill or special lessons for one of the children.

"Oh, Darling." She picked it up and held the cool green stone against her cheek. "I love it, but how can we afford it?"

"It's paid for," he grinned triumphantly. "It's been on layaway for a year and I had to make the payments in cash so there wouldn't be any checks to give me away."

That meant a whole year of careful small sacrifices Katherine knew. Where had that love gone?

It was the next year when the financial struggle had eased, she remembered. The business had started to pay off and there had been more money for the good things of life. As life became more secure, Katherine realized, it had also become less engrossing. Without the need to measure every financial step together their marriage had become routine. She couldn't place when it had become a quicksand of dull pointless days that led nowhere and had no end. She countered the boredom with a dream life. Too insulated by romantic fantasies she failed to realize that her husband was equally alone.

What had made such a change, she wondered? Perhaps they had stopped needing each other when the kids left home, Mark to his first teaching job and his own 'pad' as he called it; Julie, to the dormitory at Berkeley. There was no longer the need for a united front on the daily challenges offered by a new generation. Much of the spice of life went with them.

Strange, Katherine reflected, this is the first time I've thought of my children in this house. In her resentment at finding they had both been aware of their father's infidelity without telling her, she had shut them out. The old house was her refuge and, subconsciously, she had not allowed any of them to cross the threshold. Now, involuntarily, she had opened the door and was surprised to find much of the hard anger was gone.

Shifting restlessly in bed, Katherine wondered why these new evaluations crowded into her mind, tonight particularly. It had something to do with Paul and the emotions he aroused in her, but it was more than that. Paul's reaction on arriving had been the result of deeper changes in Katherine, herself.

Sleep finally came, but it was broken by tossing and fits of wakefulness. There were dreams, too, but she couldn't remember anything except a sense of loss, and in the morning she awoke tired.

She was dawdling over a midmorning coffee break when Dorothea came in with the mail. There had never been anything except utility bills and ads, but this morning she was startled by the two letters Dorry had placed prominently on the top of the pile. They were from Julie and from Fern, Mark's wife.

As she opened the letters, Katherine was glad they had not come while she was still so resentful. Now she could see that Mark and Julie had been right not to interfere in their parent's problems. They would have had to take sides and that would only have made things worse. A little ruefully, Katherine conceded her children had behaved more maturely than she had.

Both letters wanted news of her progress. Julie wanted to come for Christmas and bring her new boyfriend to meet her mother. Fern and Mark had happy news. Katherine would be a grandmother again in early February, and Mark had received the 'Teacher of the Year' award. They were both written in the same cheerfully casual tone and neither mentioned Charles. Katherine suspected they had consulted each other about what to write and what should not be said. She was touched by their concern, but glad it would be a while before she confronted Julie. She was probably living with the boyfriend and Katherine was not ready to deal with that yet.

As they waited Lily and Dorothea were making 'busy work' about the kitchen. Katherine's unusual preoccupation with the mail made them wonder if the letters carried bad news. When Katherine saw the concern on their faces, she put aside her letters and smiled."It's nice to hear from the family," she said, "but we've got work to do."

CHAPTER EIGHT

To Katherine's surprise, Paul was back the next morning with the expert from the furnace company. They found her in the little tower room, putting a final strip of wallpaper in place. Lacking only drapes, it was the first room to be completed from carpet to ceiling and Katherine displayed it with the pride of a mother presenting her first-born child. The men admired it and praised the view, but Paul seemed to lack enthusiasm.

"What's the matter, Paul?" Katherine asked directly. "Don't you like it?"

"You've done a beautiful job," he answered, hesitating. "I just wondered why you did this one first?"

Immediately she knew what he was thinking; why this useless cubbyhole hidden away back here? He'd have started on the front room for display to prospective buyers. Katherine had chosen it because of an instant sentimental attraction to the room, also, because it was the smallest job she could find as a starting place. Now she realized this wasn't a very professional attitude. She looked at him uncertainly, trying to think like an interior decorator, and then said the most businesslike thing she could think of.

"It's my office, of course."

A satisfied grin of approval replaced his puzzled expression. "Good thinking," he said briefly.

A cute little room with a view didn't accrue much credit, but an office apparently gave her executive standing.

The two men prowled the house all morning from root cellar to attic, measuring and tapping walls and talking about joists and clearances. It was past lunchtime when the furnace representative was finally finished. Lily had sandwiches and coffee ready for everyone.

Over lunch, Katherine tried to get a rough estimate on costs of the projected installation, but the expert was evasive. He glanced at Paul as if for help and then went into an involved explanation of why he was unable to answer. It made her very uneasy.

"Don't worry," Paul told her. "They'll send you an estimate as soon as they get it worked up."

"All right," Katherine said, adding positively, "but I want a written estimate before any work begins."

"Oh, absolutely!" the expert said.

"Naturally." Paul agreed, "but, Katy, in view of the lateness of the season, I think we ought to begin excavating right away. Regardless of who gets the bid on your furnace, they will have to have a basement to put it in and winter is just around the corner."

His words were a shock. Katherine thought of the originally suggested furnace in the Sears catalog. She knew that had gone by the board when Paul started talking about a special furnace design expert, but she was still thinking in terms of the closet-like furnace rooms generally used in California. Building a basement was something else again!

"But, Paul . . ."

Now, just don't worry about it," he said. "I'll take care of everything." It was plain he did not want to discuss it in front of the furnace representative. Reluctantly, she swallowed her protest when he added, "I'll call you later."

It was much later in the evening when he finally called and Katherine had had time to become furious. She had begun to see that she was caught in an undertaking she couldn't possibly finish. Five thousand dollars was only a drop in the bucket!

"Paul," she said angrily, "What do you think you're doing? You knew a basement would be necessary for that kind of furnace!"

"Of course, I knew it, Katy," he said. "I just took it for granted you did, too."

"Well, I didn't," she answered shortly, "and what makes it even worse is that you knew as well as I did that I didn't have the money to get involved in such a project. There's no way I could pay for building a basement."

There was a moment's silence.

"Mrs. Gardiner." Now he was angry, too. " I distinctly remember telling you that the bank would regard the Gardiner property as adequate security for an improvement loan."

"Yes, you did, but that was when we were talking about the five thousand dollars in the will."

He continued coldly, "This afternoon, my contacts at the bank assured me that your application for additional financing for a basement and installation of a heating system would be approved on your signature. I am sorry you feel you can't trust me to act in your best interests. If you no longer wish to proceed with the work, I will terminate all plans the first thing in the morning."

The finality in his voice hit her like a plunge into cold water. Why hadn't she waited for his explanation? Her temper had almost pushed her into disaster. She couldn't speak for a moment.

"N-No, Mr. Langhen," She tried to match his icy formality, but her voice was husky with tears. "I didn't realize...If the money is available, we would proceed.... I apologize . . ." Her voice almost slipped out of control and she said, "Good night," and hung up abruptly.

Katherine stood in the kitchen by the phone a few minutes, wiping away the tears. She felt so dumb! She had humiliated herself and alienated a man who had been doing everything he could to help her. She almost called him a crook, in fact. When she returned to the parlor, Dorothea looked up from her magazine anxiously. More proof of her stupidity! While she was ranting around so thoughtlessly, she had forgotten that this young woman was dependent on her actions.

"I guess I blew my top over nothing." It was a weak attempt to be offhand. "It seems Mr. Langhen has everything under control."

"Will you still need me?"

"Of course, I will! Everything is all right. I just got upset because I didn't have all the facts."

"If Mr. Langhen knew there would be enough money, why didn't he tell you before?"

It was evident Dorothea had overheard enough to understand the phone conversation. Her reasonable inquiry caught Katherine's attention.

As she sat down, she said, "That's a good question, I'd like to know the answer to it myself." Leaning back in the lumpy chair, she put her feet on the coffee table and considered the situation.

What was Paul's objective? He hadn't mentioned building a basement; he hadn't mentioned that installing the ducts around the fireplaces would raise the cost, which it obviously would. He certainly hadn't mentioned anything about more money since the initial five thousand. Then another thing came to mind. There would absolutely have to be one or more new bathrooms, and that definitely hadn't been mentioned either.

A pattern began to emerge. With understanding, Katherine's

temperature began to rise again. She was being carefully maneuvered into a huge debt to renovate the old house. Paul was minimizing or hiding the true expense. Step by step, he was guiding her in so deep she would have to finish the job so she could regain the money that had gone into it. Naturally, 'Her Realtor' would skim off a nice fat commission!

Mr. Paul Langhen was a people manipulator, and a very skillful one, too. So far she had reacted exactly as he wanted her to. Well, two could play that game! In her dating days she had been a pretty good people manipulator herself.

On realizing that there was a game involved, Katherine's spirits rose to the challenge. She really hadn't been so dumb. She had been finessed. And very neatly. A few months ago she would have backed away in panic from assuming a large personal debt. Tonight she had been made to feel grateful for the opportunity. Only for a moment did she hesitate about the consequences of playing this particular game, and then concluded that Paul's judgment in real estate matters was to be trusted. If he thought it would pay, it probably would be worth taking a chance.

Her relaxed, half asleep appearance in the chair concealed a wide-awake effort to evaluate the facts and decide on future action. The initial surge of resentment at being a pawn in someone else's game was followed by an eager desire to turn the tables. The bank's agreement to grant her a large loan needed looking into first. In no way did her situation guarantee sufficient collateral for such a loan. The property was not legally settled yet. It had to be Paul's influence. How far could she trade on that asset? It came as a surprise to realize, not only was she willing to use such an advantage, but relished the idea. Her outlook on the world certainly was changing.

Katherine's disturbing day resulted in another restless night.

Again there were dreams that were only shadows of her emotions. One clear impression remained, though. Charles was looking at her across the room and shaking his head.

"That's not my wife," he was saying. "I don't know that lady." Mostly there was just a vague awareness of being troubled and she was glad when morning came.

CHAPTER NINE

After breakfast Katherine and Dorothea helped Lily clear away the dishes. As they planned their day, a small tractor equipped for dirt moving rumbled up to the back porch. Katherine guessed work was about to begin on her basement. Paul was not going to give her time for any second thoughts on the matter.

She opened the door to greet an older man wearing a white hard hat. His younger companion carried the same type hat under his arm. They were both lean, suntanned and bore a resemblance to each other.

"I'm Clarence Yeager, Mrs. Gardiner," the older man said courteously, "and this is my son, Kenney. Mr. Paul Langhen told us last night that you needed someone to begin the excavation for your basement. Is it alright if we start this morning?"

Katherine was amused. She looked at the tractor and the large assortment of crowbars, picks and shovels they had brought and wondered what they would do if she said "no".

"That's fine with me," she grinned.

In an amazingly short time the two men, working with their assortment of hand tools had removed the stone steps. Then they gouged an opening large enough to drive their machine down into the darkness under the house. As it chugged and grunted out of sight, Katherine decided that if things were going to move this fast, it behooved her to make sure of the money to pay the bills.

"Dorry," she suggested impulsively, "I've got to go to the bank. Why don't you go with me and we'll treat ourselves to a day off?"

Dorothea was delighted and so was Lily, because Fred was home to spend the day with her.

Katherine phoned the bank first and then wasted little time in dressing for her appointment. Dress selection didn't matter because she had already decided to buy a new dress before going to the bank. In a few minutes they were on their way, leaving the men with their dirt-chewing monster growling under the house.

It was one of those glorious days when everything went exactly right. The weather was beautiful with crisp golden sunlight, and a vibrant blue sky with floating cotton puffs of clouds. The perfect dress was right in the window where it couldn't be missed and, of course, it was an exact fit. She was still overweight, but by comparison with three months ago, she felt like a fashion model. Dorothea's sincere admiration raised her self-confidence several notches and her reception at the bank sent it soaring. She received true VIP treatment. The bank manager handled the entire transaction with flattering attention.

A few careful questions confirmed Katherine's opinion that Paul was guaranteeing her loan. Not that Mr. Minyard admitted any such thing, it was more what he avoided admitting. The knowledge gave her a sense of being in control, which received a slight shock when the basement and furnace estimate appeared on the banker's desk. The total was just under fourteen thousand dollars.

"Fourteen thousand dollars?" It was both a question and an exclamation.

"We'll make the loan an even fifteen thousand in case

anything unexpected comes up."

Katherine gulped once and then plunged. "What about the bathrooms," she asked blandly. "There should be at least five to really modernize the place, four upstairs and one downstairs."

It was 'go-for-broke' testing of the limits with the most extravagant request she could think of. The banker never blinked.

"That will probably take about three thousand apiece," he said, "but we'll make it twenty
just to be sure we cover everything."

After that, Katherine simply accepted that the day was bewitched. She signed the loan papers wondering if she would wake up in the morning and find it was all a dream.

It even seemed quite in the order of things that this special day should end in a dinner date with Paul Langhen. It was late afternoon when they met in the middle of the parking lot at the grocery store. Paul's greeting was a little wary and lightly complimentary as he surveyed the new dress.

"You look mighty sharp today, Mrs. G."

Katherine detected a hint of uncertainty and her eyes glinted with satisfaction. He was usually so sure of himself, but something about her today, perhaps her air of triumph seemed to have put him a little off balance.

"Thank you, Sir. Dorothea and I have really made a day of it. We clothes shopped, window shopped and grocery shopped."

He laughed a little wryly. "I've already heard about some of your shopping."

"Things do get around in a small town." She shrugged as if borrowing thousands of dollars was no big thing in the life of a professional decorator.

"Look, Katy." He was helping to load the grocery sacks in the trunk of her car. "Why don't you have dinner with me tonight and we can talk over the plans for the house?"

Katherine, glancing at the girl, started to refuse, but Dorothea scented romance.

"Oh, go ahead, Katherine," she urged. I can take these things home. You don't need to worry about a thing!"

Katherine eyed her very steadily. "You're sure you wouldn't mind?"

For a second Dorothea paused. She hadn't thought about spending her evening alone in that big house. Then she said resolutely, "No, if I get..." she hesitated, "lonesome, I'll go visit Lily and Fred."

"Okay, Dorry. Thanks."

She turned to Paul with a teasing grin. "You better have a pocket full of cash. I'm starving."

Paul raised his eyebrows at the ultimatum.

"Don't worry, I know the chef. He'll let you wash dishes if I can't pay the bill."

Dorothea's laughter followed them as he guided Katherine across the parking lot to his car.

It was a beautiful evening Katherine thought, with all the elements required to fulfill Dorothea's most romantic fancy. The restaurant was a luxurious place of dim lights and elegant service. True to his boast, Paul was well known there and was accorded flattering VIP attention.

When the waitress asked if they would like a drink before dinner, Katherine wasn't sure. She seldom drank alcohol, and she still didn't know Paul very well.

"Yes, I would, but I don't know what to order," she decided. "I'm not familiar with cocktails. Paul, will you order for me?"

He glanced up quickly with a wicked grin.

"Certainly, if you trust me to."

A flush warmed Katherine's cheeks at the slight hint of malice behind his teasing manner. She had apologized, but apparently his ego had been bent a little. Hoping the light was too dim for him to see her color rise, she ignored the deliberate provocation.

"Of course," she smiled, "just something mild, please."

Glancing at her over the top of the menu his gray eyes were edged with little wrinkles of amusement as he ordered.

Katherine had been soaring all day on an emotional high, too elated by the day's success to realize she was getting tired. It felt good to sit down and sip a relaxing cocktail.

"Would you like to dance?" Paul asked as they waited for their food.

"I'd like to try but it's been so long I'll probably step on your toes."

"I'll take my chances," he laughed. "Lets try it."

He led the way to a rather dark, postage-stamp size dance floor where a skillful pianist, partially hidden behind palm fronds, was playing popular dance tunes as they were requested. Paul was a good dancer. After three or four steps they were moving in effortless rhythm. In spite of herself, Katherine found she was responding to the romantic setting and to Paul's charm with more pleasure than she had anticipated. She was almost sorry when the music ended.

Dropping some change into the pianist's tip box, he guided her back to the table.

"You didn't step on my toes once," he said in mock approval as they seated themselves again.

"I tried," she grinned, "but you just kept moving out of my way."

Their dinner arrived, accompanied by a light wine. It was delicious and the wine relaxed the tensions of her exciting day. Halfway through the meal she was embarrassed to find herself yawning. She hid behind her napkin pretending to cough, and tried to remember what Paul had just said about marketing the house.

He seemed more amused than piqued by her yawning inattention, although it was surely an unusual feminine reaction to his charm. He made no more serious reference to house plans, but suggested they dance again before the dessert course.

On the drive home the cool night air seemed to revive her. Paul walked her to the back porch where the kitchen light had been left burning for her return. Anticipation she hadn't experienced since she was sixteen made her pulse jump. She knew he was going to kiss her goodnight. She tried to bring back the earlier detached poise. It was totally ridiculous for a woman her age to be reacting in such an adolescent manner.

Despite all her efforts, his arms around her and the lingering pressure of his mouth left her shaken. She was a little chagrined because she knew Paul was fully aware of having ruffled her composure. They drew apart and his eyes met hers, teasing, yet questioning. Suddenly it didn't matter if he knew, because he wasn't so cool either. What he saw in her face answered his unspoken question and he grinned.

"Let's try that again!"

He kissed her again, harder than before. Then he opened the kitchen door for her. Once inside, she turned to say good night and received a light caress on the cheek and a soft, "Good night, Katy."

When Paul's car had backed out of the driveway, she put out the light and tiptoed past a sleeping Dorothea. In bed, she lay thinking over the day. It had been totally fantastic. So much had happened, it was hard to remember all the details.

Smiling, she turned toward the empty pillow on the other side and stopped in shock. Involuntarily, she had been about to share with Charles the whole adventurous day. Ambushed by a sudden despairing sense of loneliness, tears welled over onto the pillow, and Katherine cried herself to sleep. She was too dismayed by the unexpected plunge into grief to be more than vaguely annoyed that the wind was again agitating the little wooden rocker by the fireplace.

CHAPTER TEN

In the light of the bright morning sun, Katherine's tears seemed far away and so did yesterday's exalted optimism. She was still a little tired from the emotional extremes, but the feeling of having crossed an important financial bridge brought new confidence in her ability to finish the job.

As she stretched and wished for a cup of coffee, her idle gaze fell on the rocker by the fireplace. It was still. She looked at the window. It was closed. Her wandering thoughts were arrested by the realization that this had happened a number of times. Something was making that chair move at night. There must be a draft from the chimney. She got up and held her hand in front of the opening, but there was no movement of air that she could detect. A chilling thought of the little old lady with the cane contentedly rocking in the dark flashed across her mind.

A warning memory of the birds, which no longer roosted in this chimney, followed immediately. She was doing it again, letting her imagination suggest ridiculous images. There had to be a perfectly ordinary reason, probably a difference in air temperature or something. All she had to do was wait and time would offer an explanation. She shrugged away the puzzle and forgot it in planning the day's work.

Before she and Dorothea had finished breakfast, the little

tractor under the house coughed and popped, then steadied into its monotonous roar.

"I wonder if we'll fall into that hole they're digging down there?" Katherine said.

Dorothea giggled. "Kenney said his dad builds supports as he goes, so I guess we're safe enough."

The sound vibrated back and forth under their feet while Katherine concentrated on a sketch showing the new stairwell into the basement. She gave it to Mr. Yeager and then fled outside to escape the noise.

Dorothea's blonde prettiness gave her a fragile appearance, but she worked like a strong capable boy. In very short order she had mastered the use of a wide assortment of tools. Mostly through her efforts, the weather-beaten siding of the house was ready for painting. Katherine had been so busy with other tasks that she had not, until then, appreciated the immensity of Dorothea's accomplishments with scrapers and sanders.

"Dorry, you've done a tremendous job."

"Thank you, Boss."

Dorry laughingly dropped an exaggerated curtsy and then challenged, "Now, do you think we can manage to cover that whole thing with paint?"

"I don't think we can... I know we can!" Katherine boasted.

When they had gathered the painting equipment together, however, she looked at the distance from the ground to the roof and felt a little intimidated. Determined not to be shone up by her hired help, she climbed a little shakily up one end of the scaffolding that Fred had erected, while Dorothea mounted the other end. They began at the corners and worked toward each other until they met in the middle, with a good deal of paint on themselves as well as on the house.

It took most of a week to finish an undercoat of paint and Katherine, who had thought her muscle soreness was past, discovered a new set of aches and pains. If there was any movement of the rocker in her room at night she was too tired to know or care.

The next week they started the topcoat with another member added to their work crew. Much of the dirt removal work was a one-man job so Kenney Yeager often found himself with free time. He promptly attached himself to Dorothea. That was fine with her, but she allowed no slacking. If Kenney wanted to share her company, he was going to share her work.

Another pair of hands, along with Kenney's very evident desire to impress Dorothea, made the work go much faster. They never seemed to tire of the work or the endless banter that went with it. While Katherine's efforts were spurred by a cutting edge to the wind under an ominously gray sky, her assistants were inspired by their desire to outdo each other. Progress was fantastic.   As Katherine was finishing the last of the blue trim on the shutters, Paul's car crunched to a stop in the gravel driveway.

"You're a wonder," he told her, eyeing what seemed like acres of gleaming white paint. She laughed. "I had a little help from cupid."

Paul followed her gaze to where Kenney was solicitously removing a spot of paint from the tip of Dorothea's nose.

He laughed too. "Oh, Lord! Young love! That's usually more interference than help."

"I don't think so," Katherine told him thoughtfully. "The two of them did the lion's share of the work. You know Paul, Dorothea is the hardest working girl I've ever seen. Naturally Kenney wasn't going to let her show him up."

"I thought he was here to help his father." There was a slight tone of criticism in the remark.

"Certainly he is, and he's been doing that too, very satisfactorily." It did occur to her that Mr. Yeager had to go in search of his helper a couple of times, but over all, she felt her defense was justified.

"Actually it worked out just right because tomorrow they start pouring cement and then Mr. Yeager will need Kenney all the time. We were lucky to have his help this week."

"Good," Paul said rather absently, watching them cleaning equipment and putting away the ladders. Then he turned back to her with a slightly sheepish grin.

"What I really came out here for was to tell you it was too late to start this job. The weather forecast says heavy rain is due to start in a day or two."

"Heavens Paul, we didn't need the weather bureau to tell us bad weather was coming." Nor did he need to come out here to tell her that either, she thought with pleasure. He could have phoned.

"Felt it in your bones, I suppose?"

"Come here." She led him across the driveway and up to the top of a high bank on the other side. From this vantage point they could see that all but the evergreens were skeletons of their fat summer image. Early frosts and autumn winds had heaped weeds and bushes in brown mounds in the open areas. Several flocks of migratory birds fluttered and scratched for the last remaining seeds before they headed for warmer territory.

"See. They'll all be gone in a few days."

"I get your point," he admitted, "but I think you were lucky the weather held up."

"So do I," she confessed, as she sat down on the brown lawn

with her arms clasped around her knees. "We've been painting like crazy for fear it would storm before we finished."

She leaned back inspecting the glistening white expanse with satisfaction. Beyond it leaden clouds scudded across a gold streaked twilight sky. A tight mass of Chimney swifts returning to roost swooped in a high circle around and around the house. Eventually they formed a funnel, out of which little black silhouettes folded their wings and plummeted into one of the unused chimneys. They dropped with unbelievable speed, flashing out of sight with little perceptible slowing of their descent. This nightly ritual was fascinating to Katherine. Paul watched with her until the last stragglers set their wings and vanished along with the remaining streaks of color edging the dark clouds.

Katherine rose stiffly with Paul laughing at her groans, and supporting her against him a moment. She knew he was about to kiss her when Dorothea came out on the porch for an armload of firewood. It was Katherine's turn to laugh as he frowned at the interruption. He grinned back at her.

"Damned poor timing, I call it."

"Oh, I don't know." She glanced up at him provocatively. "She might have saved me from a fate worse than death!"

His eyebrows lifted and there was definitely a speculative glint in his eye as he leered exaggeratedly, "Coises, foiled again!"

He refused an invitation to supper and she waved goodbye to the receding headlights as he backed his car into the gathering darkness and turned onto the gravel road.

CHAPTER ELEVEN

All through the evening meal and cleaning up afterward, Dorothea chattered about Kenney and Paul and the happenings of the day. Amused and finally bored, Katherine was beginning to wonder if she would ever run down. Finally she did, and retired into a romantic novel Lily had given her. Then the house was so quiet Katherine felt lonely.

She prepared for bed, but it was too early for sleep. A few months ago the activities of this day would have forced her to bed in exhaustion, but now, although pleasantly tired, she was too restless to relax. She lit the fire in her room and tried to read, but couldn't concentrate. All her day had been full of noise and busy people urgently racing against an impending weather change. The contrasting quiet was a reminder of her first night in the place. The quiet seemed to deepen and so did her sense of waiting . . . listening.

Unable to sit still, Katherine began fidgeting about the room, straightening things or moving them. Fussing aimlessly at first, she soon found herself involved in a chain reaction. Moving one thing called for moving another. She forgot she was tired. Struggling to shove the heavy wardrobe to a new position, Katherine became aware of Dorothea standing in the doorway, staring.

"Katherine Gardiner! What on earth . . ." Her voice trailed off as she surveyed Katherine in a nightgown and robe, engaged in a full-scale rearrangement of the room. She looked at her watch. "I thought you'd gone to bed!"

"I did," Katherine laughed," but I couldn't sleep. What time is it?"

"After eleven thirty. You shouldn't be trying to move that big heavy thing by yourself. Let me help you."

"Gladly! It only needs to go about two feet further, but I seem to have run out of push."

Between them they managed to place the big piece of furniture to Katherine's satisfaction. She dropped wearily into the little rocker that now stood beside the door.

"Thanks, Dorry. I was just about to give up."

"Don't you think you should quit now? You look awfully tired."

"I am. I've been trying to find a stopping place for the last half hour, but there was always one more thing to do. I shouldn't have a bit of trouble going to sleep now."

Dorothea hesitated uncertainly in the doorway.

"Is there anything more I can do for you?"

"No thanks, Dorry. I'm not entirely satisfied with this arrangement, but I'm certainly not going to do any more to it tonight."

Dorothea chuckled. "I like it better this way, but it still looks more like a library than a bedroom, even without books."

"Well, of course!" Katherine studied the room. "You're right! That's what it is, after all. It should have books and easy chairs and a Boston fern." For an instant she could picture the room as it should be and the vision was more real than the bed in front of her. That's it, she thought. That's why I don't feel comfortable in here. The house doesn't like it because this room is being misused. There was that fantasy again. This strange old house seemed to have stirred up a latent imagination she never dreamed existed. It made Katherine wonder about herself. If anyone knew what she was thinking, they'd have her locked up! She'd better not even hint of such a thing to Dorothea or Lily or she'd find her help long gone.

"Goodnight," Dorothea said and Katherine yawned an answer. Dropping her robe across the foot of the bed, she slid between the sheets and reached for the lamp. With the brass chain in hand, she hesitated, studying the wooden rocker by the door. It looked out of place over there. Too weary to obey a momentary impulse to get up and move it, she put out the light. She could change it tomorrow.

In the morning, she had forgotten the passing intention and was nearly through dressing when she realized the chair was in its customary place in front of the fireplace. Her pulse skipped a beat with the discovery. Could she have been sleepwalking? That was the logical answer, but she was beginning to have a strange feeling about that chair. As she left the room with a last puzzled glance at it, she shrugged. There was no sense in mentioning something that would only cause alarm. Besides that, any ghosts or spirits here had to be friendly. For some reason beyond explanation, Katherine felt welcome in this house. Regardless of what happened, nothing here would harm her. Of that she was sure, no matter how unaccountable some happenings might appear.

However secure she may have felt, Katherine found little enthusiasm in the other members of her household when she announced her decision to move upstairs. Lily remained silent, but her wide-eyed look betrayed disturbed feelings. Dorothea argued. "There are no curtains or drapes at the windows," she said. "The bathroom is downstairs. The furniture is too heavy for us to move it upstairs."

Katherine could counter most of her objections with practical solutions. She was glad neither of the others could guess her real motive because that, she couldn't explain, even to herself. In the end she simply fell back on pure stubbornness.

"It's my house and I want my bedroom upstairs."

The girl recognized defeat, but still she tried one last argument.

"There's no bed or anything for me."

Katherine was really surprised and wondered if the words were just bluff. The last thing she had expected was that Dorothea would consent to move upstairs.

"I'll order you a bed and dresser this afternoon, if that's what you really want to do," she challenged. Then, on second thought, she said very gently, "You don't have to move up there just because I want to, Dorry. Stay downstairs if you feel more comfortable there."

Dorothea flushed. "If you're going to sleep up there, I am too." Her tone was half resentful, but her eyes glistened wetly.

She must have met with very little consideration in her life, Katherine thought. The least hint of tenderness brought her to the verge of tears. In spite of the fact that she had not done so deliberately, Katherine almost felt guilty, as if she had taken advantage of the young woman's weak spot.

Thanks, Dorry." Impulsively, she hugged her and smiled. "It is a little scary up there at night. I'll be glad to have the company."

Along with the linens they had chosen, the bed and dresser for Dorothea's room arrived on Fred's day off. With Kenney's help, which always seemed to be available, the move into the two upstairs bedrooms was accomplished in a couple of hours.

When the furniture was in place, Katherine still found the size of the Master bedroom awesome. The bed and small lamp tables seemed to have shrunk. Downstairs surrounded by all the bookshelves, the furnishings had filled the smaller room, but now they looked inadequate. The little rocking chair had been left in the library and she brought it up just to have one more piece to fill the void. It didn't help much.

She crossed the hall to see how Dorothea's room looked. It was a bit smaller, but with even less furniture, seemed equally empty. Their voices echoed from the walls.

Kenney leaned on the dresser, obviously reluctant to leave Dorothea. Katherine quickly accepted his offer to help make the rooms more livable. He brought up the tall stepladder while she and Dorothea collected bedding, curtain rods and an armload of colorful sheets. While the women made the beds and arranged their clothing in closets and dressers, Kenney put up expanding rods over the windows. They used the extra sheets as temporary drapes. Katherine had chosen color combinations that matched the new wallpaper, in shades of blue for the girl's room and yellow for hers. She finished with a couple of bright area rugs for the floors.

The change was amazing. Color made the surroundings warmer and the room spacious instead of bare. Soft folds of material absorbed sound and killed the echoes. For the first time Dorothea seemed to become reconciled to moving upstairs.

"It's the first time I ever had a room of my own," she told Katherine as they inspected their handiwork that night, "and it's so pretty!"

Privately, Katherine thought it still didn't look as feminine as most young woman would like, but it was certainly much more inviting than the makeshift arrangements that had been Dorothea's lot up to now. Katherine was beginning to understand why Dorry was so grateful for things that even teenagers considered their right, yet when it came to hard work and responsibility she possessed the attitude of a mature woman.

Thinking back to the circumstances under which she had hired the girl, Katherine realized with something of a shock that Dorothea had been the adult in that household. Liz Jenkins was as completely irresponsible and self-centered as a child and so jealous of her authority that she resented Dorry even while she depended on her earnings. The situation had taught the girl early lessons in diplomacy which she subconsciously carried into all her relationships.

With an endearing personality wrapped up in a fragile appearing blonde package, it was not surprising Kenney had plunged head over heels in love. His loved one, however, was not responding very satisfactorily. Although he was older by several years, Dorothea remained in control of the relationship. She was amused, tactful and even affectionate, but she treated him more like a big brother than a boyfriend. Watching the progress of the affair with a great deal of enjoyment, Katherine was convinced that this was the first time that Dorry had been involved with a young man. Kenney made his feelings very clear, but Katherine could not decide how the girl felt about him. At any rate, he was the subject of much of Dorothea's conversation and their horseplay enlivened the atmosphere of the old house.

With fires glowing and the dark windy night shut out by drawn drapes, their new bedrooms made a cozy oasis upstairs. Dorothea had shut all the doors to the empty rooms without referring to her former fears. In Katherine's room she stopped a moment and looked up at the smoothly replastered spot in the ceiling. Katherine noticed her action and laughed.

"Paul thought I'd be afraid to sleep in this room. He almost dared me."

"Oh, so that's it! I wondered why you were so determined to move up here."

Katherine was satisfied to let the girl's reason stand.

"Well, I couldn't let him get away with it, could I?"

Dorothea smiled back at her. "Of course not!" Then she added softly, "You like him a lot, don't you, Katherine?"

To her amazement, Katherine felt a glow warming her face. Dorry laughed triumphantly.

"You're blushing! You do like him!"

Katherine laughed too. "Yes, I do. And now suppose we talk about Kenney?"

With a prim smile Dorry answered, "Kenny is a very nice boy," and refused to say anything else about him.

Later, with the fire closed off and lights out, Katherine found herself lying very still listening for some unusual sound. Nothing stirred, however, and at last she went to sleep. Once she awoke to an awareness of dripping water and dimly realized the rains had finally started. Another time she woke up wondering where she was, but quickly remembered and went back to sleep. Except for the usual sense of dislocation brought on by strange surroundings, it was a very restful night.

CHAPTER TWELVE

Dorothea came across the hall in the morning, bubbling over with good nature and enthusiastic plans for the day's work. Katherine rapidly finished dressing and headed for the kitchen.

"Let's go get some breakfast."

"Hey, you're in a hurry!" Dorothea teased. "You must be awfully hungry."

"I'm starved!" Katherine replied, and while she really was hungry, that was not the reason for her rush. She didn't want to give the girl time to notice that the rocking chair she had carried up to her room last night was gone this morning. Although certain she knew where it was, Katherine almost held her breath as she glanced through the library door. There it sat before the fireplace, looking lonely all by itself in the room.

All through breakfast her thoughts made it difficult to follow the girl's flow of chatter. Never before had Katherine really considered whether she believed in ghosts or spirits. Now she appeared to be living with one, with something, at least, that was beyond logical explanation. There was nothing scary about it. On the contrary, the stronger the presence, the safer, more protected, Katherine felt. The spirit, or whatever it was, gave her a feeling of warmth, of belonging in this house. She knew, though, that neither of her assistants felt any such confidence. If they knew about that chair, she doubted that either of them could be persuaded to stay with her.

"Katherine?" The insistence in Dorothea's voice indicated this was not the first time she had tried for Katherine's attention.

"Sorry, Dorry, guess I was lost in my thoughts. What did you say?"

Now Dorothea seemed a little uncertain of how to ask her question.

"I just wondered . . .did . . .didn't you want that rocking chair in your room?"

Taken by surprise, Katherine hesitated then shrugged carelessly. "Oh, it just didn't seem to fit in a bedroom." When Dorothea still sat as if expecting more, she added, "It really seems more suitable for the library." Warming to her subject, she went on to explain in a pseudo- professional manner, the technique of taking one object as a theme and building the decor of a room around it.

Dorothea listened politely, but with a weighing quality in her eyes. Katherine couldn't be sure whether it came from reservations concerning someone who moved furniture around in the middle of the night, or from having a rather pedantic lecture delivered at breakfast. Anyway, the girl ventured no more questions about the chair.

It rained intermittently all day and the house was gloomy and cold. The chimneys did not draw well in the heavy air. Even a blazing fire could not throw heat the length of those cavernous rooms. Katherine looked a little wistfully at the grates of the heating vents the furnace company had already installed below the fireplaces. It would be a long time before there would be a furnace to send heat through them. The basement cement wasn't even cured yet. She was beginning to have an inkling of what really cold weather would be like with only those romantic little fireplaces for heat.

She and Dorry added sweaters over their warmest clothing and spent much of the day in the unheated rooms upstairs discussing, measuring and marking out floor plans for the new bathrooms. Katherine wished she had known she was going to be able to put the bathrooms in before they had gone to all the work of painting and papering. Now much of the work would have to be done over after the bathrooms were in.

Recklessly closing her eyes to prices, Katherine had ordered fixtures for four baths to be divided among the eight bedrooms upstairs. Already the financial waters were way over her head. If she was going to drown, Paul could just go down with her. After all, he'd pushed her in, in the first place.

With a great deal of figuring and measuring, they finally arrived at what seemed a reasonably efficient arrangement of the rooms in relation to the plumbing that would be necessary. The sheaf of scratch paper covered with plans and numbers bore little resemblance to her original paint and paper estimate. It was going to be a dream house if it didn't turn into a financial nightmare.

At last, cold and tired, they retreated to the only really warm place in the house, the kitchen, where the massive cast iron stove radiated comfort. Sitting with their feet propped up on the open door of the oven, they warmed themselves with mugs of steaming hot tea and complacent small talk. Lily came to prepare the evening meal and Katherine moved out of the way, but not out of the warmth.

While Katherine was impressed by the prospect of all those bathrooms, to Dorothea they seemed a fantasy of luxury. She compared them to the old makeshift bath off the kitchen.

"What are you going to do about that one?" she asked. "It won't look very good with all the new ones."

"No, it certainly wouldn't," Katherine agreed. "I think we'll open up that space into the tower room. That will make it large enough for a utility room with a washer and dryer. Tomorrow we'll decide on a space for a downstairs bathroom. It'll be just a sort of powder room."

She already knew where it should be placed, between the family room and the library. The decisions came without thought as if they had been made by someone else and stored away until Katherine came to carry them out. Again she had that strange feeling of being prompted to do what best suited the house, but it seemed too late to invoke caution. There was no way to stop after stepping off the end of a diving board; she had to see it through now. She wondered how far Paul would be willing to go in backing her and how far he could persuade the bank to go. The way expenses were multiplying, she stood a fair chance of finding out.

Katherine didn't sleep too well that night. The rain kept waking her and dark thoughts kept her awake for long periods. Being in debt had always frightened her. The weird behavior of that rocking chair brought questions she couldn't answer. Putting the house in shape, which had seemed so simple at first, was becoming more and more complicated. Every week there seemed to be more to do instead of less.

Paul was another problem. Were his attentions just to charm her into doing what he wanted her to? Could he really be interested in a woman her age? Was she making a fool of herself over a handsome Don Juan?

Finally, exhausted with tossing and worrying, she slept. In the morning it was still raining and her depressed mood lingered through breakfast. She could think of nothing to do. Everything had to wait now until the bathrooms and furnace were in. She tried to answer the mail from Julie and Mark, but her letters sounded complaining and she tore them up.

About ten o'clock, Dorothea was lost in her novel and
Katherine was staring gloomily out the kitchen window when Paul's
car splashed into the driveway. The gray day was suddenly much
brighter. Behind his car was a truck and she knew the furnace had
come. Paul clenched his hands over his head in a victory sign when he
saw her at the window. Then he began directing the deliverymen
around to the outside door of the basement. Her spirits climbing,
Katherine found a raincoat and a pair of gumboots and went out to
watch. Back of the house there was a sea of mud where the tractor
had churned back and forth, dragging out its loads of dirt. It even
covered the new steps. As the deliverymen slogged through it with
the dismantled furnace parts, the steps became heavily coated and
slippery and the men swore freely. Dorothea came out to watch too,
but it began to rain harder and drove the women back inside. They
went into the kitchen and watched from the kitchen window until the
empty truck backed out of sight down the driveway. Paul stayed only
long enough to tell them that the service people would be there in the
morning to put it together, and then, he too, left.

Dorothea was persuaded to leave her book long enough to
help order fixtures for the powder room and a washer and dryer.
Katherine didn't need help, but she wanted distraction to counter the
tension growing within her. Finally, she made a more determined
effort to answer her mail cheerfully and carried the letters out to the
mailbox at the edge of the lawn. For a moment she stood there in the
rain, curiously reluctant to go back inside.

"What on earth is the matter with me today?" she wondered
aloud. After all this time of feeling at ease in the house, now she
didn't want to go back inside. She was afraid, and that was ridiculous!
It had to be nerves from this everlasting rain and forced inaction.
Katherine knew she was being foolish. She told herself to stop it and

walked resolutely back into the house, but she couldn't dispel that sense of dread.

At the library door her eyes were drawn to the little wooden rocking chair. She felt a strong desire to take it up to her room, but it probably wouldn't stay and that would upset Dorothea. The sensible part of Katherine reminded her of the birds in the chimney. She decided the best thing to do was to go to bed early and sleep this whole mood off. The light was still on in Dorothea's room when Katherine fell asleep listening to the soft steady drumming of the rain.

Sometime in the night she awoke, not gradually, but instantly, and in fear. The light was out across the hall and she lay stiffly, trying to identify what had awakened her. In the dark, her eyes were wide and her skin crawled with a sense of impending danger. Listening tensely, she realized how quiet it was outside. The rain had stopped. Maybe that was what had disturbed her.

Then she heard a familiar sound, the creaking of the rocking chair. It was in her room! It seemed to be rocking faster than usual and as she listened, the tempo became more agitated. The sense of danger mounted. Unable to stand it for another second, Katherine rolled out of bed and dashed for the light switch by the door. At almost the same instant that she flipped the switch, there was a roar and chunks of plaster thudded onto the floor and the bed.

CHAPTER THIRTEEN

Katherine was still standing with trembling fingers on the light switch, staring at the shattered plaster when Dorothea burst into the room. She was stunned, partly by her narrow escape from possible injury, but even more, by the conviction that she had been awakened deliberately.

"It woke me up," she breathed to herself. "That weird chair was here in my room! It couldn't have been, but it was. I heard it."

There was barely time to recognize that thought before turning her attention to Dorothea. The girl's eyes were huge in her pale face. She stood, open-mouthed, gaping at the hole in the ceiling.

"Katherine! You could have been killed!"

"Only part of it hit the bed." Katherine was searching for reassurance for both of them. "Look. Most of it is on the floor." She started forward, but Dorothea caught her arm.

"Don't go over there, please, Katherine. More might fall."

Katherine stopped and looked up, trying to see if there were any indications of more cracks or loosened plaster. There wasn't anything she could see, but she acceded to the girl's plea to the extent of avoiding the area directly under the hole. Curiously, she picked up several clods of plaster. She was surprised to find that they were like balls of damp sand. A little pressure caused them to crumble in her hand.

"There's something wrong with this plaster. Look." She picked up more and handed some of it to the girl. "See how mealy it is? I don't think it would have hurt me if it had landed on me."

"Well, it certainly wouldn't have felt good," Dorothea objected. "It's heavy!" She crumbled a chunk in her hand and let it fall on the floor. "What makes it like that?"

"I don't know. I followed the directions exactly. Maybe it was bad plaster or something."

They speculated for a while and then decided to try to go back to sleep. Dorothea insisted that they share her bed for what was left of the night. In spite of the fact that Katherine maintained she had not been in much danger, she agreed. The possibility that more plaster could break loose over her head before morning was not a very restful prospect.

In the morning she called a local remodeling contractor. He either could not, or would not offer any explanation for the collapse of the ceiling. His attitude made her acutely uncomfortable. Although extremely courteous, he managed to leave an impression that it was the result of amateur bungling. While Katherine was very sure she had followed the instructions correctly, it was beyond question that something had gone wrong. It was humiliating to have the failure laid at her door in that gently condescending manner, but the alternative would be to blame it on the malevolent spirit Dorothea believed was responsible. The contractor's air of unctuous superiority left no room for any possibilities in between. Katherine rather tartly hired him to replaster with a secret hope that the whole ceiling would fall on his head the minute he finished the job.

When she left the room, Dorothea was lying or rather, standing-in-wait in the doorway of the other room. As persistent as a gadfly, she had tried all morning to extract a promise from Katherine that she would not reoccupy the Master bedroom. Katherine could not decide exactly how she felt about it. While she honestly believed that the real danger had been slight, the incident had been frightening.

"All right, all right!" Katherine exclaimed in exasperation, "I'll wait a week to give the plaster plenty of time to be thoroughly dry and set."

Dorothea's mouth opened and Katherine forestalled her protest.

"Then," she said firmly, "I'll think about it again!"

"But . . ."

"Dorry!" Katherine had had a trying morning. "Please drop the subject! We can talk about it again when the plaster is dry. Right now, I don't want to hear any more about it!"

"All right. I won't say anything more." Dorothea's voice was subdued; her feelings hurt by Katherine's sharp tone.

"I'm sorry, Dorry. I didn't mean to snap. It's just that I'm a little edgy today. Forgive me?"

"Of course," Dorothea assured her eagerly. "It's no wonder you're upset after . . ." she paused as a warning glint flashed in Katherine's eye. "I won't mention it again for a week," she finished quickly with a teasing grin.

Katherine smiled back; but said with mock sternness, "See that you don't!"

As they went down the back stairs into the kitchen, the girl asked, "Is there something we can work on that doesn't have to wait on the plumbing?"

"Yes, there is," Katherine answered. "I don't know what was the matter with me yesterday. I forgot there's still a little paper we didn't get to in the living room. It's right up next to the ceiling over the windows. We didn't finish stripping and sanding the bookshelves in the library either. After breakfast you take your choice and I'll do the other one."

Dorothea elected to work on the wallpaper and Katherine gathered her gloves and paint-stripping equipment in the library. The rocker was there in its usual place by the hearth. She wondered if it had been her imagination that it had been in her room before the plaster fell. Could imagination be that vivid and frightening? Then the thought of her narrow escape made her feel ungrateful. She was amused at her own foolishness. Perhaps she really was going off the deep end, but it didn't seem to matter. Her family and friends had suspected she was unbalanced when she took off on this wild project. If they knew of her growing conviction that there was a chair running around the house under its own power, they'd be certain. Picturing their reaction made her chuckle aloud.

The doorbell rang. As she went to answer it, she bestowed an affectionate pat on the curved chair back in passing.

Paul had no way of knowing, when she opened the door, that not all the enjoyment reflected in her eyes was for him. He appeared to be flattered. Two service men from the furnace company were with him. He introduced them and then turned to usher them around to the basement door. As he started down the porch steps, he looked back over his shoulder and winked at her.

"Don't go away. I've got something for you."

She waited on the porch until he came back around the corner.

"It's in the trunk." He pointed and then she saw that the trunk lid was tied in place over the protruding legs of a piece of furniture. As he was untying the rope, Kenney drove up in his father's old pickup. He rattled on past Paul's car and the service men's van and parked with the air of intending to stay a while.

"I'd have bet on Kenney," Paul grinned. "I called Mr. Yeager and asked him to open the basement stairway today so the men could get to the vent hookups tomorrow, but I was pretty sure we'd get Kenney."

When Mr. Yeager poured the new stairwell leading into the basement, he had sealed the working area with plywood to make sure there would be no premature footprints to mar his work. Katherine was eager to see the results, but all her requests had fallen on deaf ears. She felt a momentary annoyance that Paul had received immediate compliance.

Kenney walked back along the drive, reaching them just as Paul untied the last knot.

"Dad sent me over to take the plywood off the stairwell."

"Good, but would you mind helping me with this first?" Paul lifted the trunk lid and pulled a blanket from around a small office desk.

"Sure."

The two men lifted it out and set it on the dormant lawn for Katherine's inspection.

"It's solid walnut," Paul explained, "but it wasn't big enough for all my junk. It's been in storage until I could find a use for it. Think it will fit in your office?"

For a second, Katherine didn't know what to say. She had called the tower room her office just to make an impression and promptly forgotten about it. Paul's gift was more of a surprise than he knew.

"It's beautiful!" she managed at last, "But can you get it up those little narrow stairs?"

"The lady doesn't have much confidence in us, does she, Ken?"

Kenney laughed. "It's no big problem, Mrs. Gardiner, we can

handle it."

It was not actually very difficult. In a few minutes Katherine was considering the best position for the desk and wondering what she would do with an office. So far, this job had called for a lot more labor than management. The problem really didn't bother her much though, and the slight twinge of conscience was hardly noticeable over her frank delight in this new status symbol.

Kenney looked in to say 'Hi' to Dorothea and admire her steaming technique. Then he spent a little more than an hour vigorously pounding on and removing a framework of plywood enclosing the area under the main staircase. His noisy efforts finally revealed a curving stairwell completing the graceful spiral of steps from the top floor into the basement. So perfectly did it fit into the architecture that, even in cement, it gave an impression of being a part of the original house. Katherine glowed with pride. It was her design, and it was good! Maybe she should have studied architecture instead of interior decor.

A strong smell of new cement swept up the stairs and quickly permeated the whole house.

"Whew!" Katherine fanned the air with her hand.

Paul laughed at her. "That will go away when the cement is thoroughly cured," he assured her.

Everyone had to try the steps and exclaim over the large cold expanse below, but no one wanted to linger. There was nothing to see except the two workmen fitting together a jigsaw collection of furnace parts. They trooped back upstairs to find Lily in the kitchen with soup and sandwiches prepared for them. Katherine gave Paul her sketches for the bathrooms. Beyond a slight lift of his eyebrows, he made no comment and left shortly after lunch.

Kenney stayed to help Dorothea finish the job she was

working on. Between them, they made short work of the remaining paper. Then all three concentrated on Katherine's job. By the time Kenney had to leave, all the woodwork was smoothly primed for a final coat of varnish.

Katherine and Dorothea were admiring the results of their labor when there was a soft whirring sound from the direction of the fireplace accompanied by a puff of warm air. Before they could comment, one of the furnace installers appeared in the doorway.

"We're finished with the furnace, Mrs. Gardiner. If you'll come with me, I'll show you how the thermostat works."

"Already!" Katherine exclaimed. "That certainly didn't take as long as I expected."

"It's really a fairly simple set-up when everything is ready for us."

A thermostat control panel had been installed in the dining room. The installer offered a few brief instructions to Katherine with Lily and Dorothea looking over her shoulder. As soon as the workmen were gone, Katherine took immense pleasure in setting the dial as she had been shown.

"Dorry, run up and see that the vents are open in our bedrooms and closed in the others, will you?"

"Sure thing!"

Lily wore a broad smile at Katherine's pleasure, but she also wore her jacket. Not even a new furnace could tempt her to linger in the big house after dark.

"I'll be leaving now. Your supper is in the warming oven."

"I feel like I am too," joked Katherine holding her hands to the vent under the fireplace. "Thank you, Lily, I'll see you in the morning."

When Dorothea came back down stairs, she wrinkled her nose

and sniffed. "The heat feels good," she observed, "but it smells funny."

"The man said that'll go away as soon as the new wears off," Katherine promised. "Let's go eat."

CHAPTER FOURTEEN

After supper Katherine remained at the kitchen table checking and finalizing the bathroom color schemes. Dorry had retired to the old couch in the front room with her latest romance novel. The only sound in the kitchen was an intermittent humming of the furnace as it answered its automatic temperature monitor in the dining room. Katherine's attention refused to stay with color combinations. She found herself savoring the effect of a steady flow of warm air. It wasn't that the house had been so terribly cold, it was still too early for that, but it held a damp chill that the little fireplaces could not overcome. Steady heat caressed the walls, even the high dark corners. Katherine thought of a cat stretching in the sun.

She shook her head. This house did the weirdest things to her fancy! She returned to her plans, but this time her mind took off on a more unpleasant tangent. Every item on the paper turned to money. Money she owed. An impression of sinking in a morass of debt closed about her like a smothering force. Her breathing quickened. An inner trembling shook the pencil in her fingers as the sudden anxiety attack tightened its grip. Struggling for control, Katherine pushed away the papers and dropped her head on folded arms, willing herself to breathe normally and think sensibly.

I'm just tired, she thought. Paul thinks this is a good solid business venture, and so does Mr. Minyard. They wouldn't risk all that money if they weren't pretty sure of getting it back.

Gradually she fought off the panic attack, but it left her tired and a bit depressed. With her head pillowed on her arms, she drifted in half-awake, half-asleep, awareness that she should get up and go to bed. She felt too sluggish to move. Her heavy eyelids would lift reluctantly and then close again against the yellow glare of the light.

It was while they were closed that she had the impression of something like a shadow passing between her and the light. With an effort she opened her eyes and saw a small gray figure holding a black cane and moving soundlessly across the kitchen. Drowsily, Katherine recognized the little old lady she had seen in the rocking chair. She felt no surprise or alarm, but lay with her head on her arms in detached observation. The silent form crossed to the small landing at the back of the kitchen. She seemed to float up the three steps to where she paused facing the wall. Reaching out with her cane, she placed the tip of it on the baseboard and pressed down. Without a sound, a portion of the wall swung open. Dropping her cane, the old woman passed through to disappear in the darkness beyond. Katherine's eyes closed again, but only for an instant. Suddenly she was wide-awake, staring at the wall behind the landing. It was just the same grimy, ill-lighted corner as before. There was no old lady. No doorway.

Katherine was sure she hadn't been asleep, but only a dream could account for seeing a ghost walk through the kitchen wall. It really couldn't have happened. She felt a little frightened, not of anything supernatural, but of her free ranging imagination. It seemed to slip out of conscious control whenever she relaxed her guard. She wondered if the traumatic effects of a broken marriage and the fears engendered by the new existence she faced could be causing her to lose her grip on reality. She had read about people who couldn't cope with life and escaped into an imaginary world of their own. Was she one of those?

"Katherine?" Dorothea's voice startled Katherine so much that she knocked her coffee cup off the edge of the table.

"I didn't mean to scare you," the girl apologized, as she picked up the plastic mug. "I just came in to say goodnight."

"I must have been half asleep," Katherine sighed. She was aware of a tremendous relief at the interruption of her disturbing thoughts. "Guess I'd better go to bed too."

With a feeling of thankfulness for Dorry's companionship, she locked the doors and went straight up to bed. A slight sense of uneasiness lingered from her earlier thoughts, but she was tired and sleep came quickly and easily.

By daylight, Katherine found she could shrug off her experience as the result of being over tired. In addition, she resolved to forego those extra cups of late night coffee. Without waking Dorothea, she yawned her way downstairs to turn up the heat. As she moved the control with one finger, she again appreciated the advantage of a modern furnace system over building a fire every morning. Yet, to have removed all the little fireplaces would have destroyed much of the unique charm of the old mansion.

Katherine felt considerable pride in her solution as she stood looking around. It was still like a big empty barn, but now the smell of freshly sanded wood and new paint had replaced musty dampness and mildew. Even without furnishings there was warmth, a lived-in feeling in the big rooms. I'm doing a good job, she thought. I really am! It's going to have all the modern conveniences without losing any of the beauty and charm of the past.

In an aura of self-satisfaction Katherine put the coffee on to perk. It was obvious that the house would be a showplace. In a complete reversal of last night's mood, her mind was engaged in painting a roseate future of redecorating and renewing old houses. Recognizing the utopian direction of her thoughts, Katherine was smiling to herself when Dorothea came into the kitchen.

With a slightly curious expression, the girl returned the smile.

"You seem mighty happy this morning."

"Just woke up in a good mood," Katherine laughed. "The furnace works!"

As they prepared and ate breakfast, Katherine's eyes kept returning to the stair landing as if the dirty wall might explain last night's odd dream. It occurred to her that the little old lady with the cane seemed to turn up in her dreams whenever she was depressed or upset. She wondered if a psychiatrist would explain it as a Freudian reaction. Could it be that her mind produced the grandmotherly figure whenever her inner security felt threatened? Deciding this subject was beyond her, Katherine brought her attention back to the day's work

Studiously surveying the kitchen, she considered what was left to do. The wainscoting had been stripped and varnished a lighter golden shade; so had the tall cabinets. White paint had replaced the ragged wallpaper everywhere except the corner where the landing was. She felt drawn to remove this final dirty blotch from the otherwise rather antiseptic-looking room, yet strangely reluctant to begin.

"Suppose," she finally suggested, "we finish the bookshelves in the library this morning, then we can start on that corner after lunch?"

"Suits me," the girl said, reaching for her gloves. Whatever the job, it was all the same to Dorothea. Not for the first time, Katherine appreciated how lucky she was to have found such a cheerful, willing assistant. At the same time she wondered if she might be taking advantage of the fact that Dorry seemed to have missed a part of her life. She became a woman without ever having been a teenager. Other than a couple of casual movie dates with Kenney, she went nowhere, nor did she appear to want to.

Katherine pictured her own daughter in this setting. Julie would consider it the end of the world. It was Dorothea who was the oddity. Living with Liz Jenkins, Katherine speculated, might be expected to give anyone a different outlook on life.

With this thought came the realization that, for all her apparent openness and frankness, the girl had not even mentioned her pseudo mother since the first two weeks of her employment. Katherine didn't think she had visited her either.

"Dorry?"

"Yes?" The girl paused with her brush resting on the edge of the can of varnish.

"Have you seen your mother lately?"

Evidently startled, Dorothea looked down and hesitated before answering expressionlessly, "No, I haven't." Then with a direct, almost challenging look, she added, "She isn't my mother, you know."

"I know. She told me." Katherine somehow felt reproved. "I wasn't hinting that I thought you should go to see her. That's your business and I didn't mean to pry."

Dorothea gave her entire attention to varnishing the bookshelf for a minute or two. When she looked up her eyes glistened with tears.

"I didn't mean it that way, Katherine. I just meant that she really doesn't care about me. If I didn't bring in a little money, she'd be glad to get rid of me."

"I'm surprised you didn't leave a long time ago."
Dorry concentrated on her painting for a few minutes more. "I
thought I could help Virginia, but Maw said I was just trying to make
her think she was too good for her family, like I thought I was. And
then the baby came along and he was so sick I was afraid to leave him
with Maw and Ginny. As soon as he got better Maw told me to leave
him alone because it was time Ginny learned how to take care of a
baby.

"I could see there wasn't any use in my staying around any
longer. I started holding back a little money so I could get out on my
own, but Ginny found it and told Maw, and, of course, Maw took it.
She said I owed it to her because of all she had done for me.

"I did go home the first two weekends after I came here," she
offered with her eyes still on the paintbrush.

"I remember." Katherine waited.

"The first weekend, I rode my bike over. Maw took off with a
new boyfriend and left me to take care of Virginia and the baby. If I
hadn't been there, she was planning to leave Virginia alone to take
care of him. I told her I thought Ginny was too young to baby-sit. She
said, 'You don't need to worry about that 'cause you're gonna baby-
sit both of 'em.

"I tried to explain that I didn't intend to stay all night, but she
wouldn't listen. By that time she was yelling at me, 'You'll do what I
tell you to and don't you go complaining to that Gardiner woman
either, or you can just move back here where you belong. You're
gettin' too uppity since you been there anyway.'"

"You needn't be afraid of that," Katherine said. "She signed a
contract, and she has no authority anyway. As you said, she's not
your mother."

"I didn't think she could," Dorry admitted quietly, "but I

didn't want to see the kids left alone, so I stayed. Besides," there was a triumphant little smile on the girl's face, "it gave me a chance to do something I'd wanted to do for a long time. I cut and curled Virginia's hair and gave both kids a bath. I knew she'd be mad so I jumped on my bike and left before anyone was up next morning."

"Why would she be mad?" Katherine asked.

"She always said she didn't want Ginny getting any ideas about fixing herself up to attract boys.

"The next weekend when I went shopping with Lily I asked her to drop me off at home because I was worried about the kids. Maw's boyfriend was there and they'd both been drinking. He was half drunk already and started playing up to me the minute I walked through the door."

"Oh, oh!" Katherine whistled softly.

"Maw said, 'What're you doin' here?' I told her I just wanted to see if she needed me to baby-sit."

"She said, 'Well, I don't. The kids are already in bed. You don't need to hang around here just because there's a man in the house.

"It was still light out, Katherine," Dorry added angrily. "I think she just locked the kids in the bedroom to get them out of the way. I told her I wanted to call Lily to come and get me and that creep started insisting he would drive me back here." Dorothea shuddered. "Maw was mad as fire. She called me an ungrateful little tart and a lot of other things and said she was sick of having me hanging around.

"Then she started yelling at him,"'You're not gonna' drive her anywhere, she got herself here and she can just get herself back.'

"Then Jim got mad. 'You're not tellin' me what I can do.' They got so busy yelling at each other they didn't even notice when I left."

"Did you call Lily?"

"No." Dorothea's mouth twisted a little. "I just wanted to get out of there before they remembered me again."

"Dorry! How did you get home? That's almost five miles!"

"I know," the girl said, "but I only walked about a mile before Mr. Jones from the dairy farm picked me up."

"I'm certainly glad of that. It must have been getting dark by then."

"It was, but," she grimaced with repugnance as she turned to look at Katherine, "I would have walked all the way in the dark before I would get in a car with that Jim, even if he hadn't been half drunk. He's really scummy." Her shoulders twitched as if shaking off the repulsive memory.

Katherine was shocked by the tawdry story but she tactfully avoided criticizing Mrs. Jenkins.

"I'm sorry you had such a bad experience, Dorry. Have you heard from your... from Mrs. Jenkins since then?"

"No, but I don't think she wants anything to do with me as long as she's got this man living with her."

"What makes you think that?"

"I met Virginia in the grocery store about a week later and she told me Maw was still mad at me because Jim had wanted to drive me back here and that I'd better stay away."

It was apparent that Dorry was embarrassed by the unsavory conditions existing in her home. In spite of that, her eyes showed hurt at finding she was unwanted by the only family she had known. However, she evidently had come to terms with the situation without needing any help.

She is mature beyond her years, Katherine thought. I don't need to worry about her. She's a survivor. She had become very attached to the younger woman and hoped she was permanently free of that sleazy household.

While they ate lunch, Katherine studied the back staircase. It was a rather peculiar design. The first three steps led up to a square landing guarded on the left by an oak banister. On the right there was a door that opened on the back stairs, which curved up around the huge kitchen chimney. Architecturally, the landing was awkward, appearing to lead right into the blank wall. In her mind Katherine kept seeing that silent gray figure disappearing through the wall into the dark.

Her eyes traveled from the banister across the landing, then swept back again with a sudden start of recognition. On the floor, camouflaged by the oak wainscoting, an object lay against the wall. It was just where the little gray figure had dropped it last night. Her face tensed in a concentrated stare. In the bright daylight, it was plainly no shadow. Again Katherine felt that crawling sensation along her spine.

"What's the matter?" Dorothea's attention was caught by her stillness.

Katherine struggled to be casual, but in spite of herself, her voice was a little higher than usual.

"Where did that come from?"

"What?" At first Dorothea didn't see what Katherine was pointing at, then she asked, "That stick?"

"It's a cane," Katherine said. Dorothea followed her up the steps.

"I don't know where it came from. I never noticed it before." She watched, puzzled, as Katherine hesitantly approached the knobby length of wood and finally picked it up.

"What's the matter?" the girl asked again.

"Are you sure this wasn't here yesterday, Dorry?"

"I don't think so. I'm sure I would have seen it when I swept. Lily must have brought it in this morning."

"This is Lily's day off." Katherine was intently searching the baseboard along the wall.

"Maybe, I'm cracking up, but . . ." Her voice trailed off as she discovered a small circular depression in the center of the baseboard. Fighting a conviction that she was behaving foolishly, she placed the tip of the cane on the spot and pressed. For a second, nothing happened, then with all the creaking and groaning of a theatrical ghost story, part of the wall swung inward and left them staring through a dark opening framed by floating cobwebs and sifting dust.

CHAPTER FIFTEEN

Involuntarily both women stepped back as the wall moved and Katherine's hand jerked from the cane letting it clatter to the floor.

"A secret door!" Dorothea's expressive eyes were huge and her hands were pressed against her cheeks as she backed away from the opening. "How did you know about that?"

"I didn't know it was there either, Dorry." And that was the truth, Katherine thought. She'd been as startled as the girl when her dream turned to reality.

"But the cane! You knew what it was there for!"

"Just a lucky guess." Katherine felt reluctant to mention the little old lady. For months, she had vacillated between belief in a benevolent spirit and a conviction that her imagination was out of control. Now she looked at the cane and knew it was real. She could no longer doubt a presence in this strange old house nor her empathy with it, but hard common sense told her to keep her knowledge to herself.

"Let's get a flashlight and see what's in there."

While Dorothea went for the light, Katherine hurriedly applied the broom around the doorway, removing the sticky cobwebs and dislodging clouds of dust. She felt an almost breathless anticipation. Actually, this secret room could be empty, but Katherine didn't think so. There had to be a reason she had been directed to it.

Through the door, the moving beam of light picked out three steps leading down from the other side of the landing to a rough board floor.

From the landing Dorry exclaimed, "Oh, it's only a closet."

"Oh no, it isn't." Katherine was at the bottom of the steps, looking up. She reached out and touched the wooden panel at her side.

"This isn't a wall, it's a table top."

At the bottom of the steps, Dorothea measured the huge rectangle with her light. It blocked the entire room, from wall to wall.

"Wow! What a table." Standing on her tiptoes she aimed the beam over it trying to see beyond the barrier. The room was so long that the light became lost in the shadows. From what they could see, it appeared the whole area was filled with furniture, stacked and piled almost to the ceiling. There was no free space left anywhere except where they stood.

"So that's what became of the furniture!" There was triumph in Katherine's voice.

"Why do you suppose it was all stuffed away in here?" Dorothea asked.

"Albert Gardiner threatened to sell it after his father died. Mr. Worthingham thought he had carried out his threat, but it looks like his Mama was a little smarter than Albert figured. She hid it."

"How long do you think it's been here?"

"I don't know exactly, but Mr. Worthingham said Mrs. Gardiner outlived her husband almost thirty years so it must be about that long."

"Gosh!" Dorothea said. "All those years living in this empty old house! She must have really loved her furniture."

So effective was the tabletop barrier that they could not even examine their find until it was removed. To light the tunnel-like space, Katherine ran an extension cord from a kitchen outlet, and suspended a light bulb from a nail high on the wall. Then she and Dorothea began their efforts to move the table. This proved to be a lot harder than they anticipated. The expanse of solid oak had been wedged against the side of the stair banister. The massive pile of furniture behind it held it firmly in place. Climbing on a chair, Dorothea leaned across the tabletop and managed to remove a few key pieces and the oak barrier became a little more movable. In the windowless room the air was heavy and every touch disturbed a silky covering of dust as they laboriously worked their burden out through the kitchen and propped it against a dining room wall. They looked at each other and started to laugh. Both women wore a mask of dust marked by little muddy rivulets of perspiration.

Enthusiastically they went back for two massive pedestals with old-fashioned claw feet and bolted them into the bases near each end of the table. Matching chairs came next. In spite of their eager curiosity, Katherine forced herself and Dorothea to remove them methodically and clean the surface grime from each piece before they brought out another. Twelve chairs finally stood in uncrowded magnificence around the huge table. The damask seats were so desiccated that the material split at a touch, but the beautiful golden oak seemed impervious to years of dryness and dust. They were so heavy that it required a real effort to pick one up. Katherine knew they were antiques and probably very valuable, but everything was too massive for her taste. It was perfect furniture for this dining room though, with its high ceiling and air of stately formality.

"You know, it's funny." Dorry had been studying the room in silence for several minutes. "The furniture just makes the room look emptier."

Katherine examined the room again. "You're right, Dorry. I think it just draws attention to the fact that there are no drapes or rugs or pictures. It will be a beautiful room when it's properly furnished."

Driven by curiosity, the two worked through the afternoon. Straining and shoving, they moved an amazing amount of antique treasure that had been packed into that small space. Some pieces, such as a huge mahogany highboy, had to be bypassed when their combined strength could not move it an inch.

"That's going to take four men and a boy!" Katherine panted, leaning back against the wall.

"So's that." Dorry pointed to a massive chest of drawers only partly exposed by their efforts.

They found end tables, a library table, a writing desk and overstuffed chairs for the parlor. There were carved oak bed frames for all the bedrooms with matching chests and dressing tables. The box frames for the beds were still serviceable, but every featherbed had hosted mouse families much too long to be of any use.

The lovely old Victorian sofa was too long to make the turn up the stairs so they stood it on end to work it around the short banister, then tilted it through the kitchen door. When it jammed halfway through the doorway, Katherine was at the bottom of the steps and nearly resigned herself to imprisonment. To the relief of both women, a final desperate effort lifted it free.

Enthusiasm over the find supported them to a point of exhaustion before their aching muscles demanded a halt. Darkness had fallen when they finally prepared a sketchy supper. Leaving the dishes in the sink, they collapsed on the newly found parlor furniture.

All the overstuffed pieces had been securely sealed in huge quantities of brown paper with many bags of mothballs, which had protected the upholstery remarkably well. Its lovely colors had faded very little and the woolen fabric had not aged like the damask of the dining room chairs. Time had diminished the odor of the mothballs to a slight musty smell.

Tired as she was, a churning excitement would not let Katherine sit for long. She went to the phone to try for the third time to reach Paul, but his phone was still answered by an exasperating recording device. Unreasonably, this made Katherine angry. She was bursting with news of her fantastic discovery and Paul had to choose this time to be out of reach.

Disconsolately, she wandered into the library and stood leaning against the doorframe staring absently at the desk and tables. Slowly she realized the room was exactly as she had visualized it. There was no Boston fern and the bookshelves were empty, but it was now a library. The little rocking chair manifestly belonged in its place by the hearth.

Abruptly she thought of someone else who would be glad to know of her find, Mr. Worthingham. As executor he was, of course, fully aware of her activities. Katherine wasn't sure he approved, in spite of the fact that he had made no objections. He accepted her reports without comment and never mentioned either her financial or legal standing. This always made her uncomfortably aware of the insecurity of both.

When she told him her news, she was happy to detect in his voice an echo of her pleasure over old Mrs. Gardiner's triumph.

"Is it in fairly good condition?" he asked.

"Very good," she assured him. "Some of the pieces will need work, but everything considered, it's a fantastic discovery."

"How did you happen to find it?"

Katherine hesitated and then said, "Just luck, I guess." She was convinced she had been shown where to find the furniture because of her emotional identification with the house, but she was not about to admit such a bizarre possibility to anyone else.

"Katherine," It was the first time he had used her given name, "are you still nervous about the house? Does it still seem creepy to you?"

Oh no, Mr. Worthingham." Katherine drew a deep breath. "I feel... you'll think this is silly, but I feel welcome here now."

He laughed. "Every house has an atmosphere of its own. Years ago the Gardiner house had a special ambiance that used to make everyone feel welcome. Frances Gardiner would be happy to know you are restoring that atmosphere."

He thanked her for calling and his warm "Goodnight, Katherine," left her feeling exultant. She was sure that he felt his old friend would have approved of her handling of the estate. Katherine thought so, too.

As she examined the furniture and rearranged some of the pieces, she realized there would have to be carpets and drapes before even these lovely old antiques could be appreciated, as they deserved. That would be costly. So would refinishing, and there certainly would be some required. She thought about the allotment for the bathrooms. The plumbing contractor was due to start work in three days. According to his estimate, there should be some money left over. Knowing what usually happened to such estimates, Katherine was skeptical about this. It wouldn't be enough anyway she thought. If the project was to be done at all, it had to be done right and that would be extremely expensive. It might have to be left up to new owners.

Katherine became aware that she wanted desperately to be able to finish the house personally. Every step in restoring its warmth and beauty had become a step in rebuilding her strength and self-confidence. Somehow, she thought, someway, I'm going to find the money to finish this work. She went to bed with a feeling of having accepted a trust.

Paul called before they were through breakfast the next morning.

"Hi, Katy. I was out of town yesterday and just got your message this morning. Is there anything wrong?" The concern in his voice was a pleasure to Katherine, and there was a lilt in her voice when she answered.

"No, nothing wrong, but I have a surprise for you."

"Oh, oh! Good or bad?"

"Good, very good," she assured him. "I found a hidden room with all the furniture that belongs in the house."

"A hidden room." he echoed a little blankly. "Well, I'll be damned!" He was surprised, but seemed more nonplused than pleased.

"Is there anything worth saving?"

"Nearly everything," she informed him eagerly. "It's really beautiful antique stuff, Paul, and it belongs here as nothing else could. Can you come out and see for yourself?"

"Okay, okay!" He laughed at her enthusiasm. "I'm going to be tied up this morning, but I'll be out this afternoon."

On the assumption that a request from Dorothea would get special attention, Katherine asked her to call Kenney for help in moving the last heavy pieces of furniture. She was right. In a remarkably short time he appeared with two husky friends and a hundred questions about the discovery.

After his friends left, Kenney stayed to help clean and polish the lovely old wood and to look through the many drawers and cabinets. Other than an antique buttonhook and a few hairpins, they found little except brittle paper linings.

Katherine kept her own discovery of the day to herself. There was a small chair obviously meant for the library desk, but Katherine took it up to her office. As she put it in place at her desk, she bumped against a window seat. The seat slid to one side revealing a hidden nook. In it was a small red book, water stained and worn. It was a diary. As she identified the object in her hand, Katherine was swept with a sense of excitement. Without a moment's doubt, she knew it belonged to the little old lady of the rocking chair. Slipping it in her pocket, she carried it upstairs and deposited it carefully in the silky protection of her underwear drawer.

Paul came shortly after lunch with a slightly 'tongue-in-cheek' manner. He assumed Katherine had been carried away by the dramatic circumstances of her discovery. Very quickly, however, this blasé attitude was swallowed up in an enthusiasm that even surpassed hers.

He kept saying, "It's fantastic! It's unbelievable!" as they passed from room to room. He couldn't believe so much furniture could have been hidden within the house. She showed him the storage space and he stepped off the measurements with the aid of a flashlight. Finally, he conceded it was possible by transposing the footage into more familiar terms.

"It's a little wider than a furniture van," he decided, "and a van and a half long it must have been a hell of a job getting it in there.!"

"Well, I'll tell you, Mr. Langhen, it was no piece of cake getting it out, either!"

He seemed disconcerted to realize the implication of her slightly indignant attitude.

"You mean you carried all that stuff out of here?"

"Dorothea and I did," she said rather smugly, "all but the

biggest pieces. We got Kenney and a couple of his friends to help with those this morning."

"Dammit, Katy! You've no business moving heavy stuff like that! You should have hired a couple of men to do it for you."

Katherine stared at him, confused by the total irrationality of his protest. In view of the vigorous physical labor he had encouraged her to perform over the past months, his concern now seemed funny. She started to laugh at him.

He looked at her inquiringly. "What's so funny about that?"

"You just reminded me of the simple paint and clean-up job I was supposed to be able to handle all by myself."

Paul grinned a little sheepishly. "I suppose I did over-simplify things a bit," he admitted.

"Over-simplify!" she hooted. "You led me down the garden path, Paul Langhen!"

"Not yet, Katy." Paul had been standing on the landing and he began to move very deliberately down the steps with a rather wicked smirk. Her heart skipped a beat. She retreated from the bottom step, still laughing and holding up her hands as if to ward him off. He stuck the flashlight in his hip pocket, wrapped both arms around her and continued to walk her backward into the dark corner at the foot of the stair. There he proceeded to kiss her very thoroughly.

Katherine's response made her pulse beat in her ears and her whole body flush with heat. His hands moved caressingly over her back, molding her ever closer until she could hardly breathe. When he finally lifted his head and relaxed his hold slightly, she discovered her legs were weak.

Paul was breathing faster, too. He took a deep breath as if to steady himself and let it out with a soft emphatic, "Whew! You are a very impressive lady, Katherine Gardiner."

Katherine didn't know what to say. Her emotions were scrambled between an exciting sexual arousal and a truly shocking sensation of betraying Charles. While she knew there was no basis for feeling guilty, the emotion simply slipped up and stabbed her conscience by surprise. Her single status was too new and she was still reacting to thirty years of marital conditioning.

Before she had time to do more than register the swift progression of her feelings, there were footsteps in the kitchen and they heard Dorothea's voice calling her name.

"There's your guardian angel," Paul murmured pulling the flashlight from his pocket and switching it on. Still too disturbed to return a light quip, Katherine just smiled uncertainly.

"I'm coming," she answered the girl as she stepped around Paul and went up into the kitchen.

"What are we going to do for Thanksgiving?" Dorothea asked as she stepped through the door.

For a second Katherine looked at her blankly, then at Kenney standing expectantly behind her.

"Oh my gosh!" she exclaimed as the date burst on her. "That's next week!"

Dorry nodded. "Kenney has asked me to have Thanksgiving dinner with his family if it's all right with you."

"You're invited, too, Mrs. Gardiner," Kenney said quickly.

Before she could reply, Paul said very positively, "Mrs. Gardiner is having Thanksgiving dinner with me!"

"I am?"

"You are," then with a lift of his eyebrow, "aren't you?"

"I guess I am," she conceded with a laugh.

That night Katherine's sleep was restless and disturbed. She woke several times to find herself searching for the warmth of another body beside her. Her dreams were filled with disconnected scenes of tender and passionate lovemaking. They evoked a distressed sense of hurt and betrayal because it was Charles whose touch was spreading a delicious fever along her veins. Charles, who had introduced her to the mystery of sexual fulfillment that was part of the miracle of creating life. Charles, who had found a new love and no longer wanted her.

CHAPTER SIXTEEN

The contractor arrived early to start his work on the bathrooms. Katherine was expecting considerable inconvenience, but what she got was wholesale disaster.

Everything began in an orderly fashion with the supervisor condescending good-naturedly to a comparison of his blue prints with her sketches. He felt he had to explain about the walls and floors. Since they were all double, there was adequate space between them to install the pipes as neatly as if they had been part of the original building. This Katherine knew, but she listened politely as he continued to explain the blueprints.

He was interrupted by a sudden explosion of shouting outside. At the door, they were met by a very wet and muddy workman. Behind him they could see a twenty-foot geyser of water rising from the front lawn.

"We didn't break the line, Boss," he explained hastily. "It was just so badly rusted that when we uncovered it, the water pressure blew a hole in it."

Katherine didn't know where the valve was to shut off the water, but the men eventually discovered it at the driveway entrance. After several hours of checking, she was presented with the bad news. The pipe was rusted beyond use and it would not have been large enough anyway, to meet the increased demand. It would take two weeks to get new pipe and two more to install it. That meant no water in the house for a month, at least. Clearly, she could not live in the house without water. Since the same line supplied the garage apartment, Lily and Fred would have to leave also. In her depressed mood, Katherine found it difficult to hold back tears of frustration.

She called Paul to tell him she would be forced to move to a hotel to wait for repairs and he failed to understand why she should be so upset.

"For crying out loud, Katy," he remonstrated, "what's so bad about that? You can't do any more work until the bathrooms are finished anyway."

"What's so bad is that I don't have a lot of money for waterlines and hotel bills!" she snapped, incensed at his lack of sympathy.

"Katy! Unless you've been playing the horses, you should have over fifteen thousand dollars left in your account."

"That isn't my money and you know it," she said unreasonably. "That's borrowed money and it's going to take every bit of it to finish this house. I can't afford to waste a penny!"

"You're blowing this all out of proportion, Katy," he said quietly. "You've been pushing yourself too hard and a couple of weeks away from that house will probably be the best thing that could happen to you." The soothing note in his voice embarrassed her with the realization that he thought she was behaving childishly.

"I know that's probably right," she said, struggling for self-control, "but there's so much yet to do and there seems to be a new setback around every corner. I'm beginning to wonder if we'll ever finish."

"Of course, you will," he encouraged heartily. "There are always a lot of problems in dealing with old property. This is nothing unusual. Now let's forget the house for a moment. I'll make reservations for you and Dorothea at a hotel near my office if you like."

"That's too far away, Paul," she objected. "I want to be near enough to keep an eye on the work here."

"Well alright," he conceded. "There's a motel with kitchenettes about two miles from you on Park Street. Would that be satisfactory?"

She tried for cheerfulness: "Sounds perfect. Thanks, Paul."

After telling Dorothea, she located Lily who was in the kitchen supervising while Fred emptied the ashes from the range. They seemed pleased to find themselves with a holiday, especially when Katherine told them it would be a paid holiday.

The Park Street Motel was small, clean and quiet. After unpacking their suitcases, they prepared a light lunch in the tiny kitchenette and then tried to relax. In spite of her resolve to endure the delay passively, Katherine found herself dreading the forced inactivity. Every day of the past months she had accomplished more than she ever dreamed she could. Now she found herself at a dead stop. The sudden cessation of activity left her wanting to pace the floor. Dorothea seemed restless also. They finally resorted to reading. The girl's novel put her to sleep, but Katherine found it hard to concentrate on fictional problems with her own whirling in her head.

Her book forgotten, Katherine thought about Paul. He obviously found her attractive. Was it likely he might be considering altering his swinging bachelor status at this late date? What if he simply wanted an affair? She felt uncertain about entering the world of personal relationships with men again. It had been thirty years since she had met the opposite sex on this basis. The new rules of the game were much more frankly sex oriented now, she knew, and found the idea disconcerting.

Not that Katherine didn't enjoy sex. She felt a sense of loss as she remembered her passionate response to Charles in the early years of their marriage. It was something she could never be casual about. It was the ultimate expression of love for the one person she valued above all others. Could she adjust to the new moral values that made sex just a part of a pleasant evening with anyone whose company you happened to enjoy?

Dismayed by Julie's free-swinging acceptance of the new code, she had once tried to explain her feelings to her daughter. Julie's reaction was one of shock at her mother's archaic views.

"Mom, that's Victorian! People just don't think like that any more in the real world!"

Trying desperately to maintain her calm, Katherine, never the less, was swept by a feeling of outrage at this attack on one of her deepest held beliefs.

"They certainly don't," she lashed out sharply. "They think like a pack of dogs in heat!"

"Mom!" Julie recoiled as if she had been struck.

Instantly, Katherine regretted the coarse remark.

"I'm sorry, Julie, that was uncalled for and I apologize, but I think this so-called sexual freedom is wrong."

"It's not really so different than it was with your generation," Julie said resentfully, "we're just more honest about it."

"That's partly true," Katherine admitted reluctantly, "but, Honey, that doesn't necessarily make it a good thing." She paused, struggling to organize her feelings into words.

"Sex is an act of creation, and nature made it a pleasure so as to ensure the survival of the race."

"Are you saying people should only have sex when they want

babies?"

"Don't be silly, Julie! I'm only saying it's an integral part of marriage, a commitment, not just a casual social game."

"Oh my gosh, Mom! You still believe in fairies! Sex is really a healthy natural expression of affection that your generation nearly smothered in taboos and inhibitions."

Katherine was as angry as she had ever been in her life.

"Julie, you don't know what you are talking about and I don't want to hear any more!"

The exchange created a deep rift between Katherine and her daughter. Time eventually smoothed over their sharp words, but the hurt and resentment lingered, making them wary of touching on the subject again. Gradually Katherine found herself becoming reconciled to the mores of the younger generation. She didn't like it, but it was the way of the world.

Considering a possible relationship with Paul, she wondered if she could ever accept the new moral code.

Charles had! A wave of humiliation washed over her as she remembered how stupidly unsuspicious she had been. She was too old to be so naive. She was just plain dumb to be so sure Charles would never cheat on his marriage vows. The thought of having been discarded like an old pair of shoes caused her ego to curl up like a shriveled leaf.

Katherine glanced up at her reflection in the dresser mirror. I'm still attractive, she told herself resentfully. I don't look my age, either. Instead of being comforting, this last thought pinched at her conscience. She had looked her age, and more! A painfully honest person, Katherine had to admit she had really let herself go to seed. She had become complacent and fat in both body and mind. She had ceased to value her marriage and she had lost it.

Her eyes went to the mirror again thoughtfully. What would a stranger see now? Suddenly she thought about that kiss in the dark storage room and grew warm. Learning to adjust to the modern moral code with Paul might not be so very difficult. One thing she was sure of, he certainly could raise her blood pressure.

CHAPTER SEVENTEEN

Katherine was nearly asleep when the phone rang. She answered it with a slight flutter of anticipation, knowing it would be Paul.

"Did you girls get settled in okay?"

"Sure. No problems."

"Feel any better than you did?"

"More reconciled, anyway," she laughed.

"Good," he said briskly. "All hardworking executives need a vacation, so you may as well relax and enjoy it." Katherine stiffened a little. That sounded patronizing. Before she could react, Paul changed the subject.

"I've made seven-thirty dinner reservations for the three of us if you and Dorothea have no other plans."

"No," Katherine answered slowly, lifting an eyebrow at her assistant, now awake and watching her with an inquisitive expression. "We hadn't made any plans for dinner." Dorothea grinned and shook her head vigorously. Katherine was amused at her eagerness.

"We'd be delighted. Thank you, Paul."

Paul had made reservations in the dining room of one of the older conservative hotels. Dorothea had never been in such a place before. The white tablecloth and napkins and obsequious service immediately drew her quiet attention. She studied everything around her curiously.

Halfway through dinner a big man without a coat drew her attention. He and a lady were being tactfully, but firmly refused entrance to the dining room unless he donned one of the jackets hanging on a clothes tree behind the reservation desk. The largest jacket proved to be a very tight fit. The man clearly was annoyed by the whole thing. Frowning, he followed the hostess to a table near them. As he leaned forward to pull his chair closer to the table the back seam of the jacket gave under the strain and split slightly. He looked startled, then grinned at his table companion, flexed his shoulder muscles and deliberately split the seam until he was comfortable. Dorothea's amusement was such that Katherine and Paul could not help joining her smothered laughter.

As they walked out to Paul's car afterward, he winked at Katherine and asked, "Well, how did you girls like that place?"

When Dorothea didn't answer immediately, Katherine said, "The food was delicious. Didn't you think so, Dorry?"

"I thought it was very good," the girl answered, " but I didn't like the stuffed shirt atmosphere." She started to chuckle. "Neither did that man in the borrowed jacket."

Paul seemed highly entertained by her reaction.

"Well," he offered, "perhaps you'd like to choose where we go tomorrow evening?"

Dorothea started to answer and then stopped abruptly.

"Oh my gosh, I already have a date," she told them with a dismayed look at Katherine. "Kenney invited me to go skating with him at the roller rink tomorrow evening."

"When did all this happen?" Katherine asked in surprise.

"Just before the water pipe blew up. I'm sorry I forgot to tell you about it. Everything got so hectic when that happened, I forgot all about it until just now."

"Don't worry about it," Katherine smiled. "I hope you have a good time."

"Well," Paul teased as he unlocked the car door, "that's a little too strenuous for me. Katy and I will find some entertainment more suited for adults."

Dorry laughed. "And I know you'll enjoy yourself too, in spite of being such an old man."

Paul shot her a startled look before closing the car door. When they reached the motel, Dorothea got out of the car with her key in her hand.

"Thank you for a very nice evening," she told Paul formally. Then, her eyes sparkling with meaning, she looked at Katherine. "I'll leave the door unlocked for you, Katherine."

Paul watched her until the door closed behind her.

"Sometimes I don't know just how to take that young woman."

Katherine's laugh was almost a giggle. Dorothea was so obviously intent on furthering a romance between them.

"That's because she isn't a kid, Paul. She looks like one and sometimes she acts like one, but she's really a mature young woman. The atmosphere where she was raised has made her much older than her years."

"I'll take your word for it," he said without much interest.

They had reached the motel room door and he bent to kiss her goodnight. It started out as a light caress, but quickly deepened into something much more turbulent. He finally let her go reluctantly, and took a deep breath as he stepped back.

"Goodnight, Katy. I'll call you in the morning."

Dorothea was already in bed when Katherine entered the

motel room. She looked up from her book with a teasing grin.

"Paul really is a nice man, Katherine. He'd probably make a good husband."

"Maybe, but the jury is still out on that one. Dealing with a man in business isn't quite the same as living with him."

"Well, there's one sure way to find out about that," Dorry said airily.

"Shame on you," Katherine said laughing. "I don't know yet if he's all that interested or if I am either." Besides . . . the laughter faded, "I was half of a couple for so long I need to learn to be an independent person before I can consider another . . . er. . . relationship, Dorry."

Dorothea's grin disappeared. "I'm sorry, Katherine. I didn't mean to poke my nose into your business. I was just kidding."

"You've nothing to be sorry for. We're friends and I don't mind a little kidding, and after all, he is a very nice man."

Dorothea eyed her searchingly for a moment. "And handsome, too?" she ventured.

"Absolutely." Katherine burst out laughing again. "Go to sleep, Nosy," and she snapped out the light.

Paul called before they were through breakfast the next morning. "Katy, there's a place in the country I think you'll find very interesting. It was an old estate similar to your place and the owner started serving lunches to make ends meet. Now it's the most popular restaurant in the area."

"I'd like to see it, Paul, but I can't imagine turning a beautiful old home like that into a restaurant."

"You'll be surprised at this place, Katy. It still looks like someone's home. They just put tables in every room and it's like having dinner in a private house. We have reservations for seven. It's quite a drive, so I'll pick you up at five thirty."

"Okay, Paul," she agreed. "See you this evening."

Katherine found that Paul was right about the Holly Inn. It still appeared to be a gracious southern home with many holly trees gracing a spreading lawn. They were a little early and were shown to a waiting room warmed by a fireplace with tall candles on the mantle. It was like a small living room with a couch and overstuffed chairs grouped about the fireplace. The rest of the rooms had the same air of a private home. The food was delicious with a constant flow of assorted hot breads and home made jam and conserves. Katherine found it easy to picture an impoverished southern gentlewoman turning to the only way she knew to save her home.

"It's a lovely place," she told Paul on the way home. "And that food was out of this world! But I'm awfully glad we won't be doing anything like that with the Gardiner house. Maybe I'm being overly sentimental or something, but I feel that house is meant for a family with lots of children growing up in it."

"Of course, it would be ideal for a large family," Paul admitted, "but you know modern families are not so large nowadays. It might not be easy to find exactly the kind of buyer you want, Katy."

It was on the tip of her tongue to tell him that she would just wait until they found the right one when she realized her financial position didn't allow her that freedom. By the time this job was finished, a sale would be urgent, but she still felt optimistic. In spite of all the problems, Katherine was aware that much of the fear of being on her own had melted away. She felt a growing assurance in her own judgment.

"Don't worry, Paul," she answered lightly. "My crystal ball tells me the ideal buyer will be here when we are ready for him."

Paul's attentions that week contributed largely to her awakening enjoyment of life. He sought her company flatteringly often, and included Dorothea when she had no plans of her own. Dorry seemed unconscious of any age difference and her free and frank attitude sometimes shocked Katherine a little. There was nothing she hesitated to say to him, but he didn't seem to mind.

"How come an attractive man like you isn't married?" she asked once. He glanced at her as if considering whether to answer.

"I was married once in my callow youth," he admitted. "It didn't work out." His tone dropped the subject, but her curiosity wasn't satisfied.

"Haven't you met anyone else you'd like to marry since?"

The question embarrassed Katherine. In view of his constant presence all week it sounded almost like Dorry was hinting and she was horrified that he might think she was behind it.

Paul just laughed. "Nope. There are too many beautiful women in the world to be satisfied with just one," he said lightly. When Dorry didn't smile back, but continued to regard him with a sober question in her eyes, he answered more seriously. "Marriage isn't the ideal state for everyone, Dorry. Some people just find the single life preferable."

For Katherine, at least, this exchange settled the question of Paul's intentions. That's fine, she told herself defiantly. I'm not so sure I want to get married again, either, but I'm not going to sit home every night with my knitting and a cat for company. There's a lot more to life than that.

CHAPTER EIGHTEEN

After Kenney picked Dorothea up on Thanksgiving morning, Katherine went out to inspect the house. The workmen were gone for the holiday and it was quiet, but not a soothing quiet. Skeletons of the new bathroom enclosures surrounded holes punched through newly papered walls for the plumbing connections. She thought it looked more like something being torn down instead of being improved.

She found the little rocking chair covered with plaster dust. Almost apologetically, she wiped it clean and sat down for a moment, but she was too full of inner agitation to stay still for long.

When Paul first asked her to spend Thanksgiving with him Katherine had accepted an inner dare fully realizing the invitation wasn't just for dinner. With Dorothea away for the night, he seemed to feel it was to be considered a happy opportunity for their closer acquaintance.

Of course, she was willing, Katherine assured herself. She had already come to that decision earlier. She was even eager, but also churning with conflicts and uncertainties. It would be the first time she had ever gone to bed with a man other than Charles. Paul was so sophisticated. Would a man of his wide experience find her a satisfactory bed partner?

Katherine wandered up the steps to the little tower room and gazed unseeingly through the tall windows, as she grappled with a tiny cobweb of guilt, a sense of breaking her marriage vows. That was ridiculous. She certainly owed nothing more to Charles, and her children had their own lives. Already, that other part of her life seemed far away. Perhaps after tonight it would quit haunting her entirely.

On her way out she stopped at the library door for a moment and stood looking at the motionless rocker. With the sensation of being reminded of a neglected friendship, she recalled the scuffed red diary lying forgotten at the back of her lingerie drawer. A glance at her watch showed she was already short of time to get back to the motel and dress for her dinner date, but a sense of urgency pulled her upstairs. She quickly retrieved the moldy little volume and tucked it in her bag before hurrying out of the house.

Hiding the book in her motel bureau, she showered and quickly dressed in a new sheer wool afternoon dress purchased for the occasion. As her final preparation, she rather self-consciously folded her prettiest nightgown with its matching peignoir and placed it in the briefcase doing duty as an overnight bag.

Since Kenney's mother had invited Dorothea to stay overnight, the small suitcase had gone with the first packer. Not that Dorry hadn't offered her first chance at it. The matter of fact way she accepted the probability that Katherine would spend the night elsewhere left no doubt that she was older than her years.

Katherine was glad she had hurried when Paul arrived earlier than the specified time. "Your watch is fast," she observed gravely as she opened the door.

"I notice you're ready," he countered, adding as he stepped through the door, "and you look beautiful!"

She barely had time for a conventional "Thank you" when he swept her close and kissed her heartily. He laughed at having taken her by surprise and kissed her again, slowly and gently this time.

"M - m - m -!" He rubbed his cheek against her temple. "I could keep this up indefinitely, but the turkey would be burned to a crisp. Ready to go?"

"You bet! After all your promises, I'm expecting something really special." Only half joking he had boasted all week of his superior qualifications as a chef.

"Lady, I never promise what I can't deliver."

He picked up her coat from the chair and held it for her. Then he lifted her handbag with a facetious grimace at its weight. "Is this everything?"

She let the question hang in the air for a moment and then committed herself.

"Yes, except for that briefcase. I've got my toothbrush in there."

"That's all?" He lifted his eyebrows with an insinuating grin and she added quickly, "Among other things."

The evening breeze was sharp, carrying a hint of the heavy frost that would cover the ground in the morning. There was a spicy smell of wood smoke in the air that almost predicted the crackling fire that welcomed them in the living room fireplace. Relinquishing her coat to Paul, she moved gratefully to its warmth.

"Gosh, that feels good! It almost feels like snow out there."

He turned from hanging her coat in the closet. "I wouldn't be surprised to see it snow any day now. Would you like a cocktail or a glass of champagne?"

"Champagne, please."

While he was getting the drinks, she looked around admiring the spacious room tastefully decorated in muted colors. It was really beautiful. Delicious aromas coming from the kitchen drew her in that direction. A glance confirmed her suspicion that it would be an efficient laboratory for meal preparation.

He wouldn't let her do anything. Even the table in the little dinette was already set with gleaming china and crystal and tall candles casting a flickering light on the scene. It's perfect, she thought, almost like something out of 'House Beautiful Magazine'. There was a theatrical air about it. It was too perfect; really more like a stage setting than a bachelor apartment.

Paul filled their plates from a buffet-like arrangement in the kitchen and served them with a flourish. The food was excellent. He was every bit as good a cook as he had claimed.

"If you ever get tired of selling houses," Katherine teased him, "you could make a darned good living as a gourmet chef."

"Thank you, Madam," he bowed.

She was amused to see that he felt her lavish praise was deserved. He was obviously well pleased with himself. Nor would he let her help afterward.

When she declared herself unable to eat another bite, he insisted on seating her on the couch before a coffee table loaded with fruitcake, liqueurs and a pot of rich aromatic coffee.

In a remarkably short time, she heard the dishwasher start and he joined her on the couch. For a while they sat talking quietly, sipping coffee and absorbing the ebb and swell of stereo melody softly filling the apartment.

Paul was leaning forward, elbows on his knees, gazing into the glowing coals and pulling thoughtfully on his pipe. The position accented his handsome profile. She thought he resembled an actor posing for a publicity photo and wondered if the pose was deliberate. He was one of the most attractive men she had ever met and, an unwelcome inner voice pointed out, one of the smoothest operators.

Such a masterly host must have had a lot of practice. Katherine couldn't help wondering how many other women had been wined and dined in this romantic setting. How much did he really care? Was she just another number on his coup stick?

Her thoughts were interrupted when Paul got up to put another log on the fire. Curiously she watched him roll up the fur rug in front of the fireplace. He flipped a switch and a lilting dance tune filled the room. Holding out his hand he asked, "Shall we dance? It's a small space, but there's nobody else to bump into."

She went into his arms eagerly, closing her mind to everything except the pleasure of their bodies moving to the rhythm of the music. They danced and drank coffee laced with Creme de Cocoa. Talk shifted from food to movies and finally, the house. Paul said he thought he could sell it for a sum that made her head spin more than the liqueur did.

Gradually the suspense grew within her as she waited for an indication that the time had come for the evening's finale. Paul seemed in no hurry. He kissed her occasionally and teased her when she missed a step because he was holding her too tightly. Then when Katherine stifled a small yawn, she realized that he too, had been waiting. He accepted her yawn as a signal and kissed her lingeringly.

"It's getting late," he said softly. "You get first crack at the bathroom while I put these cups and things in the kitchen."

Paul certainly knew every move in the game, she reflected as she retrieved her briefcase. Of course, she recognized that it probably was only a game he was playing, but that was all right. According to Julie, she didn't know what the score was and Paul was certainly capable of teaching her. She thought of the way the blood had pounded in her ears when he kissed her in the darkness of the secret room, but realized her heart was beating faster now from pure nervousness. She left the protection of the bathroom reluctantly.

Paul was waiting, suavely handsome in silk pajamas and matching robe. He saw she was shivering and threw back the bed covers.

"Hey, you're cold as ice! Let's get you tucked in." He put her dressing gown on a chair, then drew the comforter up to her chin. "I'll be back in a moment and warm you up properly."

He was as good as his word, but by that time Katherine was already drowsily warm and when he drew her close to him she was aware of a distressing preference for sleep. As he kissed her, gently at first, and then with increasing desire, she waited expectantly for his practiced caresses to set the slow fire burning in her veins, but nothing happened. Instead his touch became slightly distasteful and the realization dawned that she had committed herself to something she really didn't want. The whole seductive evening, carefully planned to raise her to the peak of romantic desire, had simply turned her off, cold.

She wanted to tell him to stop, to let her get up and go back to the motel, but she couldn't. She had agreed to it, even invited it, and she wouldn't be playing fair to back out at this stage. She tried desperately to feign rising passion, her only real desire being to end this whole thing as quickly as possible. Her thoughts were chaotic. Why couldn't she respond? She liked Paul. They were both free to love as they wished, but all the willingness was in her mind. Her body refused to cooperate. Then suddenly her frustration was crowned with humiliation. Paul knew!

He drew back to see her face. "What's wrong, Katy?"

She started to say "Nothing", but to her horror, felt tears slipping down her flushed cheeks.

"I don't know," she admitted miserably. "I want to, but I just can't."

He didn't seem to know what to say.

"I'm sorry, Paul," she almost wailed as the tears came in earnest.

He patted her gently on the shoulder as he drew away. "It's all right, Katy, don't cry." Handing her a box of tissues from the nightstand, he fumbled for a cigarette for himself. Then he sat on the edge of the bed with his back to her and drew deeply on the cigarette.

"I'm really sorry, Paul," she sniffed. "I don't know what's the matter with me."

"Don't worry, Katy, it's all right." He smoked in silence for a moment. "Would you like me to take you back to the motel?"

It seemed inconsiderate to ask him to dress and take her back so late, but the situation now was so uncomfortable, Katherine felt she couldn't get away fast enough.

"I hate to put you to so much trouble, but it might be best if I went."

"It's no trouble, if that's what you want," was the brief answer as he stubbed out his cigarette and began to pull his trousers on over his pajamas. Katherine fled to the bathroom to dress.

In the car there was little conversation until they were almost to the motel.

"Katy?"

"Yes?"

He hesitated as if searching for words and finally asked, "Have you ever thought about getting professional help?"

Her head came up sharply. "For what?"

"For your problem. It's nothing to be ashamed of, Katy. A good psychiatrist can sometimes change your whole perspective. Didn't your husband ever suggest treatment?"

Understanding came with a jolt. He thought she was frigid and had evidently jumped to the conclusion that this was the reason her husband had divorced her. For a moment, Katherine was furious. Ironically, when every other interest in their marriage was gone, this was still the one plateau on which they had continued to communicate, until Charles discovered his new love, at any rate. She opened her mouth to set him straight, then stopped.

What could she say? "I'm not frigid, you just don't turn me on." That would be spiteful. It wasn't Paul's fault she had attempted something she couldn't carry through. Let him think what he wanted to. The evening had probably been a little hard on his self-esteem, anyway.

"No, he didn't," she answered shortly, "and I would rather not talk about it."

"All right, Katy, but if you ever change your mind, I know a good man in that field." She thought his voice reflected the pity one might feel for a cripple. Their arrival at the motel saved her from the necessity of replying. Thankfully, she made good her escape as quickly as courtesy would permit.

The cold impersonal motel room was a relief to her chaotic feelings. She turned up the heat and threw herself into a large chair without removing her coat. It seemed she had been away for days, instead of a few hours, so great was the tumult of emotions still rioting through her mind. The evening had started out in such great anticipation and ended in mortification. She didn't even want to see Paul again, yet it wasn't his fault. He'd been truly a gentleman. It was something within her.

Maybe Julie was right, Katherine thought. Perhaps I am inhibited by the taboos of my generation. The more she thought about it, however, the less satisfactory that explanation seemed. Then, as the room grew warm and her mind quieted, the truth presented itself with a simplicity that made her aware of how really far afield she had wandered.

She wasn't really looking for sex, just reassurance for her battered ego. She wanted proof that she was still attractive, that someone wanted her. Paul was a handsome man whose attentions were immensely flattering, but he was also very shallow. "A pretty face with naught behind it" she thought with a glimmer of humor. He had transformed sex from an act of love to an artfully performed physical exercise. That was what had really turned her off. Perhaps, in the future her physical needs would change her reactions, but for now, she knew that she was not ready for a light-hearted roll in the hay.

A little stiffly, Katherine pushed herself out of the overstuffed chair and prepared for bed. Reflection led her down several avenues of thought. One was regret because she knew that the tingle of excitement in her relationship with Paul was gone. Ruefully, she realized it had now been replaced with a slight desire to laugh at his rather overdone arrangements for a night of seduction. Another was the question of how to handle the awkwardness that was likely to attend their next meeting. Her mental wrestling was ended by a glance at her watch. It was four o'clock. Wearily she turned out the light, reserving the solution for tomorrow.

In any event, it was not Katherine, but the telephone that was to direct the next move in her life.

CHAPTER NINETEEN

Katherine awoke to the realization that the phone had been ringing for some time before she was able to struggle out of the mists to answer it. Too sleep drugged to absorb the impact of the message, her answers were woodenly mechanical at first. It wasn't until her son's voice was raised in anxiety that the fog began to disperse.

"Mom! Are you all right? You don't sound like yourself."

"I'm all right, Mark, just sleepy. I didn't get to bed until late."

"It must have been some party! I called every hour until two o'clock!"

Mark sounded put out and Katherine felt guilty when she realized she had subconsciously shut all thoughts of her family out of her mind. Memories of previous holidays together were painful reminders of things she had lost.

"I'm sorry, Mark," she said somewhat defensively. "I was invited out and I had no way of knowing you were going to call."

"Oh hell, Mom! I'm sorry. I didn't mean to gripe and I hope you had a good time, but this has been a pretty bad night for us."

By now, Katherine was fully awake and the tremor in Mark's voice was transmitted so clearly that sudden fear almost stopped her breathing.

"What's. . ." She had to stop and clear her throat to regain control of her voice. "What's wrong, Mark?"

"We lost the baby, Mom." There were tears in Mark's voice. "Fern tripped coming down the stairs and fell all the way to the bottom. The doctor says she will be all right, but they couldn't save the baby."

"Oh Mark!" Tears were running down Katherine's cheeks. "I'm so sorry, dear. I'm so very sorry. How seriously was Fern hurt?"

"It was pretty bad, Mom." She heard him blow his nose. "She'll be in the hospital a few more days and then will have to stay in bed for a while when she gets home." There was a pause.

"Mom?"

"Yes?"

"Can you come and help out for a while, until Fern gets on her feet again?"

"Of course," she answered. There was no way Katherine could have said no, nor did she want to. In addition to being needed, there would be something practical to do besides sitting around a motel room until she could get back to her project. As she packed her suitcase and tried to anticipate all the loose ends to be met in case of a prolonged stay, Katherine could not let herself think of Mark. The pain in his voice echoed in her heart until she could do nothing but cry. Firmly she forced her thoughts to the details of the work she was leaving behind.

As long as the bathrooms were unfinished, she could do nothing more at the house. Because of the holidays it appeared it would take much longer than the originally estimated time to finish this part of the project. So far, there had been nothing to complain of in the contractor's work. Probably things could safely be left in his hands. Dorothea could keep her informed and would be all right at the motel until her return.

She could rely on Paul too, she thought with some

embarrassment. Last night's fiasco had somehow shrunk in importance. It might cause some strain in their future relationship, but now was not the time to worry about it.

It also occurred to Katherine that she was likely to run into Charles during such a family emergency. What if Betty should be with him? She had only seen the woman once and she certainly didn't want to see her again. For an instant, Katherine felt a vengeful desire to express her contempt if she ever met the harpy face to face. Then she laughed derisively. I'd behave like a lady, if it killed me, she told herself. After all, Paul says I'm inhibited.

On second thought, she knew there was little likelihood of such a meeting. Charles would never willingly expose her or himself to such a confrontation.

Every time she allowed herself to dwell on Mark and Fern, the tears would start again so she kept reaching for other things to busy her mind. The packing was quickly finished and she was lucky enough to get a plane reservation at noon. She was reluctant to call Paul too early and there was no telling when Dorothea would return. Time seemed to crawl by.

At nine o'clock, Katherine walked down to the motel office to pay her bill and let them know she would be gone for several weeks. The clerk's manner was so solicitous, she suspected he had listened in on her phone call, but it didn't matter. She also made arrangements for Dorothea to stay at the motel indefinitely. Even in the unlikely event that the plumbing should be finished before her return, she knew the girl would not want to return to the house alone.

On her return to the room, Katherine dialed Paul's number.

"Paul," she said when he answered, "I have to go back to California."

"Katy," he protested, "I told you it's all right. I won't . . ."

"This has nothing to do with last night, Paul," she cut in. "It's a family emergency. My son needs me." Her voice was crisper than she intended with the effort to keep her emotions under control.

"Your son needs you?" he repeated in a tone of disbelief.

Katherine took a deep breath and said steadily, "My daughter-in-law tripped and fell down a flight of stairs and they lost their baby."

"I'm very sorry to hear that, Katy." His stiffness vanished with understanding. "How long will you be gone?"

"I don't know. Several weeks, at least."

On learning that she already had her reservation, he offered to drive her to the airport and Katherine accepted. She was surprised and relieved that he seemed to want to return to their earlier friendly relationship.

Just before Paul came to pick her up, Dorothea returned, glowing with the pleasure of her first old-fashioned family Thanksgiving. There was no need to ask if she had enjoyed herself, it shone from her face. Katherine hated to prick the bubble of joy surrounding her, but there was no help for it.

Dorothea's quick compassion was warming and Katherine really didn't need her earnest assurances to feel that the efficient young woman could manage by herself. For someone who appeared so fragile, she was remarkably strong and levelheaded. Besides, there was no doubt that Paul would keep an eye on her.

Dorothea rode with them to the airport and stayed by Katherine's side in a very protective manner while Katherine picked up the ticket and checked her baggage. The after holiday rush had not yet swelled the usual crowds of travelers and they moved easily through to the boarding gate. At the moment of parting, Paul pressed her hand sympathetically between his, but did not offer to kiss her.

Dorothea's eyes held a slightly puzzled expression at the reserved quality of his actions. That young lady certainly didn't miss much Katherine thought wryly as she slid into her seat and tightened the seat belt.

Exhausted both emotionally and physically by the events of the past twenty-four hours, Katherine slept most of the way to Chicago where she changed planes and went right back to sleep. She was awakened by the buzz of activity at mealtime, but could eat little of what was served. However, that little, along with two cups of coffee, revived her energy a bit and she was awake when the plane landed at Los Angeles.

CHAPTER TWENTY

In the terminal she spied Mark immediately, but he did not see Katherine before she had jostled her way through the crowd to his side. Then he eyed her uncertainly until she spoke.

"Hello, Mark," she said soberly.

"Mom!" He seemed astounded as he grabbed her in a rough bear hug. "Wow! Have you changed! I didn't recognize you."

Katherine laughed through tears. "I didn't think you did." She kissed his brown cheek, noting with concern that he looked a bit haggard. His clothes were wrinkled and his curly brown hair uncombed.

"Are you all right, Mark? And how is Fern?"

"I'm fine," he said quietly, "but it's going to be a while before Fern is on her feet again." His face crumpled a little. "I'm so glad you're here, Mom. We really need you."

Before she could answer someone bumped into her and knocked her against Mark. "Let's get out of this damn mob," he growled angrily as he steadied her. "The baggage area is that way."

They threaded their way along the busy corridors and pushed up to the baggage carousel. It wasn't a long wait. As they came around, Katherine grabbed her small bag and pointed out the big one to Mark. When they reached the parking lot, he stowed the suitcases in the trunk of the car and ushered her into the front seat.

The traffic monopolized his attention until they hit the steady speed of the freeway. Katherine's heart ached for her first-born as he told of the frightening hours of not knowing how badly Fern was hurt and the tragic loss of the girl baby they had so hoped for.

"It's harder on Fern than it is on me," he concluded unhappily. "She wanted a little girl so badly, but I can't help just being thankful I still have her and the boys."

"I'm sure she must feel the same way, Mark," his mother said earnestly. "It's just that it will take longer for her to accept the loss because her body needs to heal first."

"I suppose you're right." Mark drove in silence for a while, then Katherine was aware of a deeply speculative glance in her direction. She knew what was coming before he spoke banteringly.

"Mom, you look about twenty years younger. What did you do, find the fountain of youth, or have your face lifted or something?"

"Mostly or something," she chuckled, thinking of the aching muscles and the nights she was too tired to remember going to bed. "You're very flattering, thank you, but all I've really done is lose weight and cut my hair."

"Any new interest in your life?" he fished.

"Several," she admitted lightly. "Mainly a house that haunts me, and a 'Don Juan' I've been dating."

Her eyes danced at the knowing expression on his face. The part about the house slid right by him and he was only aware that his mother had admitted to an interest in another man. It was just as well, she thought. If she tried to explain about the house he wouldn't believe her and he'd probably be upset if he did.

It was a long drive to Mark's house and Katherine was tired when the little car came to a stop in his neatly graveled driveway. She climbed out stiffly, rubbing her back and yawning. As Mark started to put his key in the lock, the front door was opened from inside by a plump gray-haired woman who looked like she must be someone's mother.

"I heard you drive in," she smiled.

He introduced her as Mrs. James, his next-door neighbor. She stayed only long enough to assure him that every thing had gone well in his absence.

"The boys wanted to wait up for you, but I reminded them that they had promised you they would go to bed when I told them to, so they did. They're such good boys, Mark, it's never any trouble to take care of them."

After she was gone, Mark took his mother's luggage to her room. They stopped for a peep at the two little look-alikes who appeared to Katherine to be carbon copies of their Dad at that age.

"They're beautiful," she whispered. "They look like the little angels you put on the top of the Christmas tree."

"Hold that thought," he grinned as he closed the door. "This will be the last time you'll see them in that light. They're really a pair of live wires, in spite of Mrs. James flattery."

The live wires failed to live up to their reputation the next morning. They stole silently into the kitchen, stopping just inside the doorway to watch Katherine trying to familiarize herself with things by helping to prepare breakfast. She knew better than to rush them and only smiled, "Good morning," before turning back to butter the toast.

Mark turned from his pan of scrambled eggs. "Well, hello, Sleepyheads! Are you hungry?" They both nodded solemnly.

"Good," he said. "It's almost ready."

Without taking his eyes off Katherine, the four-year old asked,

"Did Gramma come?"

"Why sure, Mark," his Dad answered. "That's Gramma. Don't you remember? She came and stayed with us when Ricky was born."

Unwilling to admit there was anything he couldn't remember, Mark nodded uncertainly

"That was a long time ago, wasn't it, Mark?" Katherine encouraged with a sly look at Mark senior. "Even your Daddy didn't remember me very well."

"That's for sure," her son admitted. He scooped up chunky eighteen-month-old Ricky for deposit in his highchair where he was served scrambled eggs and bacon on a paper plate.

"Ricky gets a paper plate 'cause he breaks things," Mark informed his grandmother. She appreciated the information a few minutes later. The baby was awkwardly using his fork with his right hand and alternating with fingered bites from his left hand as they fell on his bib. Presently he decided he'd had enough. With a motion too quick to stop, he swept the plate, fork and an empty plastic cup from the high chair tray and leaned over curiously to survey the results on the floor.

"It's messy," his father said apologetically as he picked things up, "but he has just started to use a fork and he screams his head off if anyone tries to feed him."

Katherine's memory involuntarily put Julie in what might have been that same highchair, an upended bowl on her head with great gobs of oatmeal and milk running down her surprised face. Babies didn't change, she thought, no matter what happened in the adult world around them.

By the time breakfast was over, both youngsters had lost much of their shyness and Mark was apparently beginning to place her. As they were leaving the table he asked, "Gramma, where's Grampa?"

She felt her son's eyes on her and answered very casually, "Oh, he couldn't come. He had to work." That seemed ambiguous enough to fit whatever the child might understand about the situation. Anyway, it satisfied him.

Shortly after the children were dressed, Mrs. James reappeared to take them to her house while Mark drove Katherine to the hospital to visit Fern. They found her sitting up in bed, wan, but determinedly cheerful and eager to get home. She was so glad to see Katherine that they both cried a little.

"I think," she told them in a rather shaky voice, "that if I can be busy and have other things to think about I'll get back to normal a lot faster. It's so depressing having to lie here with nothing to do but think about what happened."

"Okay, Honey," her husband said gently. "We'll get you home as soon as we can, but it depends on what the doctor says. I'll talk to him before we leave."

To divert the ready tears of illness, Katherine started to talk about the house. She gave a humorous twist to the setbacks and the mistakes caused by her inexperience and deliberately minimized the exhausting physical cost her progress had demanded. Nor would she discuss the financial cost either, in spite of her son's obvious curiosity, but shrugged it off with a casual reference to a "little money that went with the house."

"And then to cap everything," Katherine was beginning to see the funny side of her own tale, "the water pipe burst and there was this huge geyser spraying water about twenty feet in the air. The workmen got all wet and muddy and we couldn't find where to shut the water off."

Just then, the doctor walked in to find his patient laughing heartily. Plainly approving, he acknowledged Mark's introduction of his mother.

"You're the kind of medicine my patient needs," he smiled. "Now, I must ask you both to wait outside for a few minutes while I see how she's doing."

"Don't run away," Fern grinned. "I might get to go home with you." When they were allowed to return, however, her face reflected disappointment.

"She is doing very well," the doctor explained quietly to Mark, "but there is still some elevation of temperature and no appetite. I will check again on Monday and if the temperature is normal, she can go home Tuesday morning."

At Fern's immediate exclamation of pleasure, he turned to Katherine with a smile.

"That is, she can if she will stay in bed for a week and not try to get up and resume her normal household duties." His eyes were on Katherine questioningly and Katherine's reply was emphatic.

"She'll stay in bed if we have to sit on her!"

Shortly after the doctor left, they prepared to take their leave also. Fern protested, but it was plain that she was tiring rapidly. Katherine walked out to the car while Mark said good-bye to her.

"I'm glad they're keeping her a couple more days," Mark said on the way home. "She seems so weak yet."

"She'll be all right, Mark," his mother reassured him. "It just takes time."

"I know," he sighed. "I'm sure glad you're here, Mom."

Then he grinned at a new thought. "By the way, Fern didn't recognize you either, when we first walked in. At least, she said she wouldn't have if she hadn't known you were coming with me. For just a second before she saw me behind you, she wondered who that pretty stranger was."

Katherine laughed, but she didn't quite know if she liked it. While such compliments were highly flattering, she really didn't feel all that different. Momentarily it made her aware that she had lost her familiar niche in life and brought the rather bleak thought that her new life might find her permanently outside of the family circle.

Except for an afternoon visit to the hospital, most of Sunday was spent getting reacquainted with her grandchildren and learning where things were kept in the house. Her son seemed to be a very relaxed parent and their attitude indicated that the children were as used to their father's care as their mother's. As soon as she learned the primary rule (I'd rather do it myself), young Mark admitted her to the charmed circle of his companionship, but Ricky held her at arms length. He was friendly, but went to his father for anything he wanted. Mark rocked him to sleep in front of the television that night as Katherine watched. She wondered if he would be difficult tomorrow when his dad went to work and left him in her care.

CHAPTER TWENTY-ONE

As she expected, Ricky howled indignantly the next morning when he realized his father was preparing to leave without him. It didn't seem to bother Mark. He picked the little boy up, hugged and kissed him, then put him down on the couch next to his brother. He kissed the older boy too and said, "Take care of your little brother and help Gramma today, okay?"

"I will," he promised with his arm barring Ricky's efforts to get down and return to his father.

"I'll see you tonight," Mark told them. Then raising his voice so Katherine could hear him over Ricky's noisy protests, he added, "He'll quiet down when I'm gone."

To her surprise, he was right. The car had barely rolled clear of the driveway when the baby's furious screams subsided and he approached her with upheld hands and pouting lower lip. Katherine picked him up and he cuddled tightly against her, snuggling gently on her neck. Tenderly, she hugged the little body closer and backed into a rocking chair for a few moments of soothing motion. He remained quite still until he was satisfied he had received his proper mead of sympathy and then began to squirm to get down.

"You little faker," she laughed. "That was quite a show."

Mark, who had remained a serious wide-eyed observer of the proceedings, now decided the time had come for him to assume his responsibilities.

"C'mon Ricky," he said coaxingly. "Let's go play with the blocks." His grievance forgotten, Ricky headed eagerly for the toy box in the corner without a backward glance. Thankfully Katherine turned her attention to the kitchen.

She had just finished the breakfast dishes when she found Mark standing beside her.

"Gramma."

"What?"

"Ricky pooped."

Sure enough, Ricky's diaper needed changing. She cleaned him up and proceeded to straighten the boy's bedroom with Mark helpfully superintending the job. Then it was midmorning snack time, then time for Ricky's morning nap, then lunchtime. A little after lunch she put both boys down for their afternoon nap. As she came out of the bedroom, Katherine glanced at her watch and realized it was time to see what was available for the evening meal.

The kitchen was well stocked. She planned her menu, and made a few preliminary preparations before dropping onto the couch with a slightly weary sigh. She had forgotten just what a full time job childcare really was. If today was typical, she certainly wasn't going to find time hanging heavily on her hands. With her feet resting comfortably on a hassock, Katherine picked up the morning paper. The newsprint soon blurred and she was dozing when a soft little voice reached her.

"Gramma. Gramma? Are you asleep?"

She opened her eyes to find Mark, his little face still flushed with sleep, standing in front of her clutching one of his storybooks.

"Just resting my eyes," she smiled at him.

"Oh. Would you read me a story?"

"Sure. Come on up here." She patted the couch at her side.

The book was more pictures with captions than story, and when it was finished, her grandson looked at her seriously and said, "Gramma?"

"What, Honey?"

"Are you my new Gramma or my old one?"

The question was a shock with its suggestion that she was being replaced, but it also indicated that Charles had not yet introduced his new wife into the family circle.

"Your old one," she said quietly. "I've been your grandmother since you were born."

He considered a moment. "Are you getting old?"

Katherine wasn't sure where that came in, but she admitted, "I'm afraid so."

"When you get real old, will you grow into a tree?"

His grandmother chuckled. "I don't think so. I don't want to be a tree."

"Well, I'm going to be a tree when I get old," he informed her loftily. Conversation finished, he slid off the couch and strolled over to his toy box, leaving her with a sense of having been given a brief glance through the looking glass with 'Alice in Wonderland'.

That evening, Mark, Sr. brought home the welcome news that Fern would be released from the hospital in the morning. The boys were ecstatic. Their joy was a bit dampened when they found they were not going to the hospital with their dad, but they were partly reconciled when Gramma said she wasn't either.

"We have to get everything ready for your Mama to come home and I'm going to need your help to do it right."

Katherine wondered how much Ricky really understood and how much of his behavior was merely a reflection of his brother's.

There seemed to be some mystic form of communication between them that was denied to the grown ups. Mark often served as interpreter both ways.

There was one subject, though, on which no one could communicate with Ricky. His need for his mother's presence exceeded his understanding of her need for rest. For the first couple of days after Fern got home, Katherine was hard put to sidetrack the child's demands so her patient could sleep. Then as Fern gained the strength to entertain and talk to him occasionally, he lost the fear that his mother might disappear again and grew more willing to leave her side part of the time.

With every minute filled, Katherine found the days running together in her mind until she wasn't always sure what day it was. The pressure eased a little in the second week when Fern started to be up and about. At first, she merely watched or entertained the boys, then gradually assumed the lighter household tasks. Katherine was able to spend more time just enjoying the children and becoming reacquainted with her daughter-in-law. She was unaware of how long she had been there until the house began to be filled with Christmas secrets and plans for holiday decorations.

Charles had not been to see Fern since she came home, but he had phoned several times to ask about her. Katherine had not happened to answer any of these calls. Charles was seldom mentioned in her presence and Betty never. As she became aware of how carefully they were avoiding anything they thought might upset her, Katherine regretted her free-swinging blame at the time her marriage had broken up. Mark was obviously trying to walk a chalk line of neutrality. Regardless of her personal feelings, she didn't want to create any problems for him. Besides, those feelings had changed a great deal since then. In a rather stumbling fashion, Katherine tried to explain this to Fern.

"I wasn't happy, but I probably would never have made any effort to change the situation. In a way I still loved Charles. Whenever I considered divorce it seemed such a cruel thing to do to him. I couldn't charge him with mistreating me because he never did, but I was so bored. The years ahead looked so dreary I sometimes thought I'd rather be dead.

"When Charles said he wanted a divorce I was absolutely shell shocked. It was so humiliating that he could prefer someone else. For a long time I'd been dreaming of what I could do if I were free. All of a sudden, I was free and it was like being dunked in cold water."

"Be careful what you wish for, you might get it," Fern quoted.

"Right," Katherine smiled wryly. "It was hard on my ego to realize he preferred another woman, but it was really for the best."

Her daughter-in-law looked at her doubtfully.

"I'm not just being a Pollyanna," Katherine laughed. "For the first time in years, I'm thinking and acting independently. I'm a whole intelligent person with ideas and talent.

"In an ironic sort of way, I seem to be back at the crossroads where I chose marriage over a career. Fate's rubbing my nose in it and saying, 'All right, you've been daydreaming about the fantastic career you could have had, now prove it!'"

"And Fern," she looked up, her eyes shining with excitement, "I *am* proving it! That house is going to be a showplace! But more than that, it's starting to have a special air, a warm friendly ambiance that wraps itself around you . . ." She stopped, laughing at her own enthusiasm.

"Now, I'm bragging! But I do feel good about it and the bank and my real estate agent are backing my judgment."

Fern had been hanging on Katherine's words, clearly moved by what she heard. Now there was a sudden concentration of interest in her expression.

"What does the bank. . .?" Just then the phone rang and Katherine jumped up to answer it, thankful for the interruption. That was a slip. She didn't want to be questioned about money just yet.

"Gardiner residence," she said pleasantly.

"Hello . . . Katherine?" It was Charles.

CHAPTER TWENTY-TWO

For an instant, all that registered was surprise that she should have forgotten the warm romantic timbre of Charles' voice on the phone. Her answer was cool and formal.

"Hello Charles," she said. "How are you?"

"I'm fine," he returned uncertainly. "How are you?"

"I'm fine," she echoed politely and stood waiting for him to continue. There was a moment of silence and she received the impression that he didn't quite know what to say next. It gave her a gratifying sense of being in command of the situation.

Finally, he said uncomfortably, "I called to ask about Fern. How is she?"

"She seems to be doing very well. Would you like to talk to her?"

"If it's convenient, please."

"Just a moment." Gathering the long cord in one hand, Katherine carried the phone over to place it in Fern's lap.

"Charles would like to talk to you."

Not wanting to eavesdrop, she headed for the kitchen to pour a fresh cup of coffee spiced with the savor of a minor triumph. There was considerable satisfaction in the knowledge that Charles was the one whose poise was disturbed by the unexpected contact. She stood at the kitchen window, sipping coffee and watching her grandsons at play in the back yard until their mother called her back to the living room. Fern was holding her hand tightly over the mouthpiece of the phone.

"He'd like to drop by for a visit tonight. Would you mind?"

Katherine hesitated. "Just Charles?"

"Yes."

"No, I don't mind."

Fern studied her face intently. "I can make some excuse if you would rather not see him," she offered.

"No, it would be childish to try to avoid him. Anyway, I honestly don't think it will bother me all that much."

If Fern was not entirely convinced, she accepted Katherine's decision at face value and cordially invited her father-in-law to come for a visit.

At the supper table that night, Mark flashed his wife a slightly startled look when he learned of his father's impending visit. Even though she had tried to explain to Fern, Katherine realized they were still apprehensive. It struck her as being a little funny. What did they expect her to do, start a donnybrook in the middle of their living room?

No, she decided, they were probably afraid she would burst into tears every time Charles spoke to her. They had not recognized that her changed appearance was only a surface indication of her inner changes.

She was not about to cry about a man who didn't want her. When she thought about the smothering boredom of their last few years together she drew a genuine breath of relief that she felt alive again. The past months had often been depressing, lonely and exhausting, but they had also been months of accomplishment and excitement. It was exhilarating to discover that she could handle life on her own. There was no way to know what lay ahead, but there was definitely a wasteland behind her.

The stunned look on Charles face when Katherine walked into the living room that evening was all she could have hoped for.

"Hello, Charles." There was malicious glee in her eyes, but her voice was totally casual. "Are you all ready for Christmas?"

"Yes . . . No . . . not quite yet." He finished shrugging out of his coat and handed it to Mark without taking his eyes from her. "You certainly have changed, Katherine."

So have you, she thought. His suit was new with a shirt and tie of much brighter colors than he used to wear, but there was something else and it took a moment to discover what it was. The little bald spot on top was gone. Charles was wearing a hairpiece! The realization brought a little spark of resentment that he had gone so far to cater to this younger woman. Then she wanted to laugh.

She couldn't have been more gracious as she answered, "Thank you, Charles." Then with a little laugh, she added, "At least, I hope that was a complement."

Uncomfortable under her amused glance, he answered shortly, "Of course it was,"and then turned solicitously to Fern.

"I just wanted to tell you how sorry I was about your accident. How are you feeling?"

"I'm feeling fine, Dad," she assured him. "All the bumps and bruises are healing, but I'm still not getting out very much. Fighting my way through the Christmas shoppers is a little too much to tackle yet."

This remark led to a rather banal discussion of the heavy traffic and crowded stores while Mark busied himself serving eggnog in little crystal cups. When he sat down again there was a lull in the conversation. Charles ventured a comment on the sunny California weather.

"It is beautiful," Katherine conceded, "but it doesn't seem much like Christmas." Then she, who had spent practically all of her life in California, proceeded to describe a Christmas card picture of the snowy Maryland countryside. It was shamelessly plagiarized, with enthusiasm, from Dorothea's most recent letter.

"I thought you didn't like cold weather," Charles said a little sourly.

She shrugged one shoulder carelessly. "I've had to learn to like a lot of new things lately." She was pleased to see his color heighten. For the second time, she realized she had succeeded in irritating him. Katherine liked the sensation of keeping him off balance. Revenge might be an unworthy emotion, but her conscience didn't bother her a bit.

Charles didn't stay long after they finished the eggnog and his departure left three rather quiet people behind. Fern started to help Katherine gather the cups but Ricky woke up, his fussiness indicating a wet diaper.

"You take care of him," Mark told her. "I'll help wash up."

Mark was quiet as they straightened the kitchen and Katherine felt a little guilty. She knew that her vengeful gibes at Charles had made him uncomfortable.

"Mark," she said tentatively.

"What?"

"Do you think Fern is strong enough to cope with things now?"

Her son turned from the sink to confront her.

"Why?"

"Well, I thought perhaps I ought to get back to my work."

"Mom." Mark paused searching carefully for words to express his thoughts. "I don't know what we would have done without your help. If you really feel you must go, I don't want to impose on you. Fern probably could manage, but we were hoping you'd want to spend Christmas with us."

"What if your father wants to bring his new wife to visit?" her tone was bitter. "That might make a really uncomfortable situation for everyone because I don't mind admitting I would resent it."

"I thought that was it," he said quietly. "If that should happen, we'd find a way to handle it, but it's not likely it will."

"What makes you so sure?"

"I'm not sure of what they might be planning. Dad's been avoiding me, but I know they're not married yet."

"They aren't! But Mark, that's why he wanted me to go to Reno. He was in such a tearing hurry for a divorce so they could get married."

"I know. But when you told him that if he wanted a divorce, he could go to Reno and get it himself, he filed here instead. He said he couldn't afford that much time away from his business."

"But here, it takes a year for the final decree, doesn't it?"

"That's right. Didn't you get the papers?"

"No. Not a thing." There was shock and dismay in her voice as she asked, "Then technically, we're still married?"

"That's right, Mom. I'm sorry, I thought you would have received all the legal junk by now."

"Well, I haven't!" She slammed one of the crystal cups down on the counter. Mark rescued the cup and asked curiously, "Are you in any special hurry to be free, Mom?"

"No, not really," she answered, "but it's been hard getting used to the idea that my marriage was a closed chapter in my life and now I find it actually isn't. It's just a little upsetting, that's all Mark," she explained with the conviction of having made the understatement of the year.

Katherine went to bed when the kitchen was straightened up, but sleep evaded her. She had admitted to being a little upset, but in reality her hard won tranquility had been deeply disturbed. Her air of casual indifference toward Charles had grown painfully out of the belief that this part of her life was irretrievably buried in the past. She was angry that she should still find herself tied to the source of the hurt and humiliation she had struggled so hard to overcome. It was like a second betrayal.

Out of her frustration, she deliberately sent her thoughts to the old house in Maryland, invoking the sense of pride and self-confidence gained from her accomplishments within its walls. Remembering the soothing rhythm of wooden rockers on the floor at night, she finally grew drowsy. At the edge of the gathering shadows of sleep, there materialized a reminder to read the neglected diary in the morning.

CHAPTER TWENTY-THREE

That last thought was still in Katherine's mind when she woke up, but the opportunity wasn't there. She had overslept and so had Mark. The resultant turmoil demanded an 'all hands on deck' effort to send the man of the house out on time. By then, the boys were up and the morning's work began. It wasn't until after lunch, when Fern had joined the boys for their afternoon nap, that she could retire to the privacy of her bedroom again. With a mounting sense of anticipation, she retrieved the leather book from her suitcase and lay down to read.

The writing was fine and spidery on yellowed paper that crackled with age. In places the ink was faded and pale, yet legible. Glancing through the pages, Katherine discovered it was not a day-to-day diary she held in her hands, but a journal spanning most of the writer's lifetime.

On the title page was written with a proud flourish: '*Property of Frances Grace Gardiner*, *February 14*, 1910. Opposite this inside the front cover was glued a gift card with an inscription in broad masculine strokes. It said, ***"To our valentine on her seventeenth birthday. With love, Mama and Papa"***

In the beginning the pages carried a meticulous record of the daily happenings in a happy young girl's life. As the novelty wore off, only the most interesting things were deemed worth recording. By her eighteenth birthday her writing showed a growing maturity as well as romantic interest in the local boys. Her social circle offered light-hearted parties and balls with few serious thoughts to disturb the even tenor of country life. There was no hint that things might not always be so.

A month after her eighteenth birthday there was a brief stark entry.

March 21, 1911 Papa died today of pneumonia. I am worried about Mama.

That she had good reason to worry was borne out by the next brief entry made four days later.

March 25, 1911 Mama died today. The doctor said it was heart failure from the strain of losing Papa. I am so alone and I do not know how I shall manage.

Katherine's heart went out to this girl whose words so mirrored what she had felt in that same house. The writer had barely started on the adventure of living and Katherine had already traveled much of her allotted span, but that same devastation of spirit materialized in front of that small fireplace. I felt her sympathy and understanding, she thought. That's why I dreamed about her. Following those words of despair the diary apparently was ignored until the next blow fell.

April 5, 1911 Papa's solicitor was here today. He told me Papa was in debt to cousin Andrew Gardiner, who has filed a claim on our property. I do not believe it.

April 15, 1911 Papa's solicitor was here again today. Cousin Andrew has sent proof of his claim, but says he does not want to turn me out of my home. He suggested that it would solve the problem if I would marry Patrick or James since Andrew, Jr. already has a wife. He wants to give us my home for a wedding present! How very generous of him!

May 2, 1911 Mr. Johnson was here again today. He visited Papa's cousins last month and he advises me to consider the marriage offer. He says they are nice and he thinks Papa would approve. I doubt it. They were such ruffians! The last time they were here, James tried to feed my canary to the cat and Patrick pushed me in the fishpond. Mr. Johnson says Patrick is coming to see me next week. I dread it.

May 8, 1911 I was never so surprised in my life! Patrick is the most understanding and sensitive man I have ever met. He has grown very handsome, too. He said he never meant to push me in the pond, it was an accident.

May 15, 1911- It is arranged. We will be married by the justice of the peace next month. I will not have a real wedding because I am in mourning, but Cousin Andrew says it is necessary to secure my future now. I suspect the future of the estate is of equal interest to him, but I find I don't mind too much as Patrick is a great comfort to me.

As the entries continued, it was obvious that Patrick was a great deal more than comfort. Far from its touted purpose as a practical necessity, the marriage bloomed into a fairytale romance. It was love at first sight (as adults) between two people who were perfect in each other's eyes.

Katherine was suddenly flooded with glowing memories of her own magic bridal days, that precious time of unalloyed happiness she was sure would last forever. It was a shock to discover that such a state of golden bliss could simply be gone without a trace. She felt a poignant sense of loss of that young love with its flowers and laughter and sharing which seemed as far in the past as the old love story in her hands.

Slowly the book slid out of her fingers and Katherine found herself thinking dispassionately about her marriage. Again, she tried to put a mental finger on a time or event that had begun the change. But it defied analysis.

She couldn't point to anything specific, no violent quarrels, no betrayals, not until the end, anyway. Their relationship had just decayed with age like the old house in Maryland she thought. Too bad lives couldn't be refurbished with paint and paper in the same way.

Katherine was awakened by loud shushing noises as her grandsons tried to keep each other from waking her.

"It's all right," she laughed. "Grandma's awake."

"Are you going to get up?" Mark asked.

"Yes, I'm going to help your mother get supper ready for you and your daddy."

"Oh." They came in and stood watching solemnly as she put the diary away in a dresser drawer and ran a comb through her hair. As she watched the curious little faces in the mirror, Katherine came to a decision. Come what may, she would stay through the holidays. If Charles had the bad taste to bring his girlfriend around she wasn't going to let it bother her. The legal details might not be final, but their relationship was over and she was going to enjoy building a new life of her own. Fleetingly, it occurred to her that she had told herself this quite often over the past months.

As Christmas drew nearer, the holiday tempo stepped up and Katherine found herself involved in the festivities. Mark and Fern were a very popular couple and their friends began including her in their invitations. At first, she tried to evade them by offering to baby-sit, but her son and daughter-in-law firmly vetoed this arrangement. As she became socially active, it was inevitable that she should cross paths with friends from the pre-Betty days. Her pride carried her past the first reluctance to expose herself to people who knew she had been cast aside. It soon became evident that her younger appearance and self-confidence drew envy, not pity. She found herself in demand and enjoyed it tremendously. She lunched and shopped with her women friends, parrying their curiosity with a shrug and a quip. At evening affairs, Katherine found it amusing that some of them watched her closely when she danced with their spouses.

It was not too surprising when Harry Marten suggested that there was something missing from her life that he'd be glad to supply. In the fifteen years she'd known the Martens, he'd always been flagrantly unfaithful to Joyce. The surprise was to find him so certain that she would be filled with a burning desire to get a man in her bed. He was holding her so tightly that it was difficult to dance and she pushed him away.

"Harry, I don't need anything in my life that you could supply, besides, Joyce is my friend."

He tried to pull her closer again. "Don't worry about that, she'd never know."

"I don't care if she wouldn't know. I don't want an affair with you or anyone else!"

"You don't need to be coy with me, Katherine. I understand a woman's needs."

Katherine's face reddened as his hand slid down to her buttock. She abruptly whirled away from him to leave the dance floor, only to bump squarely into Charles.

"May I cut in?" he asked as if unaware of the anger in her face, and without waiting for a reply, quickly waltzed her away from Harry.

"Thanks!" she said shortly into his shoulder.

"You're welcome." They circled the room in silence.

Still without looking up, she said, "He's a creep," in a slightly shaken voice.

"I know." There seemed to be a faint hint of amusement in his tone and Katherine looked up resentfully, but his expression was bland.

Looking around, she asked with unmistakable sarcasm, "Where's the girl of your dreams tonight?"

"Betty's not here," he said stiffening. Then the music ended and he escorted her across the room to the group around Mark and Fern. With an air of having done his duty, he said goodnight to everyone and left immediately.

Fern appeared tired, and for Katherine, the evening had lost much of its zest. She was glad to find her son and his wife were ready to leave the party.

While Mark took the baby-sitter home, Fern came to Katherine's room, clearly attempting to read something into the fact that Katherine and Charles had danced together. She was disappointed when Katherine casually explained that Harry Marten made a pass at her and Charles had come to the rescue.

"He may be having second thoughts about his situation," Fern persisted.

"Well, that would just be too damn bad!" Katherine returned sharply. Then she apologized. "Sorry, I didn't mean to snap at you. It's just that Charles can't help being a gentleman. He'd have rescued anyone caught by that human octopus."

In spite of her attempt to be casual Katherine realized her voice sounded a bit flat. She decided she must be extra tired tonight. Fern seemed to come to the same conclusion because she dropped the subject and went to her own room.

Katherine undressed moodily. The incident with Harry had been upsetting. It had been considerate of Charles to step in and ungracious of her to prod him about Betty. She felt depressed and wondered if she might be coming down with something. Perhaps it had been a mistake to stay here. She'd be glad when the holidays were over and she could get back to Maryland and finish her job. She heard Mark come back and finally fell asleep.

CHAPTER TWENTY-FOUR

The depressed mood was still there when Katherine awoke. She felt restless and impatient and the noise level at the breakfast table rasped on her nerves. She was in the kitchen loading the dishwasher when the phone rang.

"It's for you," Fern called. "It's Charles."

"Okay." Reluctant, yet curious, Katherine picked up the kitchen extension.

"Hello."

"Katherine?"

"Yes?" Her tone was impersonal.

"Would you do me a favor?"

He's certainly got his nerve, she thought, and her voice was contentious as she asked, "What sort of favor?"

"Well, you've been around the boys a lot lately and you know what they like. Would you help me pick out their Christmas presents? I'm not asking the favor for myself, Katherine, but for the boys. Christmas is so special for children."

Katherine was strongly tempted to tell him to get Betty to help him. Then she realized she didn't want her grandchildren to be grateful to that person for anything. She couldn't refuse.

"All right, Charles," she said smothering her resentment. "When would you like to do it?"

They made arrangements for him to pick her up at ten-thirty. By the time Katherine had finished the kitchen chores, informed her very curious daughter-in-law of her plans, and dressed to go out, Charles was in the front room with Fern and his grandsons. As she came in, Charles was searching for a diplomatic way to refuse to take the two eager little boys with him. Their mother ended his problem with a firm statement.

"No, you cannot go with Grampa today." Then she turned to him. "Do you have plans for Christmas Eve?"

Charles looked first at Katherine, then at the boys.

"Well no," he said uncertainly, "nothing definite."

"Then, we'll expect you for dinner, won't we, boys?"

Ricky nodded, but Mark was not so easily appeased.

"When's Christmas Eve, Grampa?"

"Tomorrow night," Charles informed him. "Will that be all right with you?"

"But where are you and Gramma going?"

"Nowhere that would be any fun for you, Mark. We have some shopping to do."

"Oh, okay." Mark gave up with obvious reluctance and Charles glanced at his watch.

"We'd better be on our way," he said. "I'll see you boys tomorrow night."

In the car, conversation was awkward and formal. The heavy traffic demanded most of Charles attention. Katherine was wondering if Christmas Eve would be so uncomfortable and if he really had no plans for that evening. It seemed entirely possible that Fern had blackmailed him with his sad-faced grandchildren.

When they finally parked and worked their way into the crowds of last minute shoppers, Katherine found it necessary to take a firm grip on Charles' arm to keep from being swept away. She also found herself responding to the holiday excitement around her. For the first time it really began to feel like Christmas.

Not only had the children's gifts been neglected, Charles had not bought anything for any of the people on his list. Without quite knowing how it happened, Katherine found herself struggling from store to store at his side, haggling over what was appropriate, and gradually filling their arms with packages. With only a couple of names left on his list, Katherine sagged onto a chair in front of a department store jewelry counter.

"Charles, I'm exhausted. If you want any more help from me, you're going to have to feed me."

He looked at the time. "No wonder! It's after two. Let's park this load and go eat."

They put the packages in the trunk of the car and chose a small cafe in the mall. Since it was past the lunch hour, there was no waiting and Katherine slid into her chair with a grateful sigh.

"I'm sorry," Charles said ruefully. "You should have spoken sooner."

"I kept thinking you'd surely get hungry pretty soon."

He shook his head. "I guess all I had on my mind was getting finished while I had some help."

They talked easily through lunch in the relaxed atmosphere of mutual accomplishment. Katherine gave him a lighthearted account of her work on the house in Maryland. He mentioned that his business had done well this year. The only time the conversation became personal was when he surprised her with news of Julie.

"She called last night. She'll be here sometime tomorrow and wanted to know if it was all right if she invited a boy to stay through

Christmas break." Katherine's eyebrows went up and Charles grinned.

"She made it very clear he would use Mark's old room so no one's sense of propriety would be offended."

Katherine laughed. "That's a switch. She told me she planned to spend the holidays with a girlfriend's family."

"I think," he said quietly, "that was before she knew you were planning to spend Christmas here."

Suddenly Katherine was very glad she had stayed. It would probably be the last time they would all be together for a Yule holiday. She couldn't help wondering if Charles was going to have any trouble with Betty if he spent the holidays with his family. It would serve him right if he did.

All she said was, "I'm glad she changed her mind. Shall we get on with the rest of your shopping?"

The last two choices proved difficult to shop for. They were both tired when the last packages joined the brightly wrapped jumble in the trunk. There was very little conversation on the way home, and Charles declined to come in.

"I'll see everybody tomorrow," he said. "Just tell Fern I'll be bringing two more for dinner. I hope she has enough food."

"I will," Katherine smiled, "but I don't think you need to worry."

He caught her hand as she opened the car door. "Katy, I really appreciate your help today. It was very generous of you."

This was too personal for Katherine and she jerked her hand away and slid her feet out of the door.

"Thanks," she said dryly," but it's no big deal. They're my family, too, in case you've forgotten." She slammed the car door in sudden irritation.

Fern poked her head out of the kitchen as she heard the front door open.

"Well? So you're finally home. I was about to call 'Search and Rescue' to find you."   "They'd never have found us in that mob. It's wild out there." Katherine sank on the couch and kicked off her shoes. "Sorry to be so late, but we just finished."

"Just finished what?" Fern stepped in the doorway with a paring knife in one hand and a tomato in the other. "Don't try to tell me it takes all day to buy a couple of presents for two kids."

"Of course not." Katherine gave an exasperated sigh. "That was just the bait. He hadn't bought one single gift. We did his entire Christmas shopping today."

"For heaven's sake, Katherine! Why did you go along with it? Under the circumstances, that was pretty shabby of him."

"Well," Katherine admitted a little sheepishly, "he didn't actually ask me to. The kids names were at the top of the list and I was sucker enough to start suggesting things for the others."

Fern laughed. "You're soft in the head, Katherine Gardiner."

"I'm afraid you're right. Was there any mail for me today?"

"No, but you had two phone calls; one from that girl who works for you and one from your real-estate agent."

Katherine frowned. "That sounds like trouble. I'd better call them back."

She tried Dorothea first but the motel manager said she was out. When she tried Paul's number she found he had left a message for her.

"Don't worry about Dorry's call. She just got a little panicky. I'll call you as soon as I take care of it."

CHAPTER TWENTY-FIVE

Katherine lay in bed later than usual the next morning, reluctant to face the day. The conviction that she had allowed herself to be used by Charles was mortifying. The part that bothered her most was that she had really enjoyed his company the whole afternoon. That made her feel vulnerable. In retrospect this morning it seemed incomprehensible that he could be so self-centered as to have asked her help. The past months had blasted her out of an indolent backwater into an exciting new life stream. She couldn't let Charles undermine her new strength. She was in control of her life and intended to stay that way.

Thoughts of being in control reminded her of yesterday's phone calls. She tried to reach Paul again. There was no answer at his apartment and his business phone still carried the same message from last night. Dorry wasn't available either. So much for being in control of things! Battling a sense of impotence she realized she was just going to have to wait until Paul called her.

With an odd feeling of turning to a friend Katherine located the old leather diary in her dresser. Resolutely, she relaxed against the pillows and retreated from her dejection into its musty smelling pages.

At first, Katherine thought her marker was in the wrong place because the new entries began five years after the glowing honeymoon days. Finally she concluded it had probably been put away as part of childhood when Frances Grace married. She had apparently begun confiding in it again as an outlet for her deep disappointment when she failed to conceive a child. Her writing revealed a changed personality as her desire for a child became an obsession that overshadowed everything else. It was sporadic, depressed and sometimes angry.

The entries began late in 1915 and the only December entry was brief and blotched with tears.

Dec. 2, 1915 I wish we could stay home this Christmas. I hate going to Cousin Andrew's. All of Patrick's brothers and sisters will be there with their children. I alone am barren.

The next entry was nearly three months later.

Feb. 14, 1916 Patrick is such a good person. He gave me a lovely ring for my birthday. I asked him if he wished he had married someone else who could have given him children and he said he didn't. Of course, he wouldn't admit it if he did. It broke my heart to see him with the children at Christmas. He'd make such a wonderful father.

There were only two more entries for that year.

July 20, 1916 We finally got to see Dr. Murchison, but he simply agreed with all the others. There is no physical reason that I should fail to conceive. He was embarrassed when I broke down and cried, but he was very understanding.

Oct.15, 1916 I asked Patrick again if he would consider adoption, but he is very set against it. He said he does not want someone else's child. He only wants ours, his and mine. I left the room so he would not see me cry. I cry so easily these days.

I don't need this, Katherine thought. About to put the book away, she turned the next page to find a date splashed across the top of the page and underlined twice. It fairly shouted with joy.

Mar.10, 1917 I'm pregnant! After all these years, I'm pregnant! Dr. White laughed at me because I thought I had the flu, but I don't care. My prayers have been answered and I know it will be the son Patrick has always wanted. He has promised to buy me a rocking chair this week.

The page blurred a bit as Katherine's heart echoed the mystical joy of discovering the first new life growing within her body. Sounds outside her door told her the rest of the household was gathering in the kitchen for breakfast. She knew it was time to get up and help, but the diary now held her in suspense.

The pregnancy was a difficult one with the constant threat of a miscarriage. Katherine leafed rapidly through emotional accounts that ranged from dark despair to buoyant hope. At last, the end of the ordeal was solemnly recorded in very shaky handwriting.

Aug.10, 1917 Today, our son, Albert Leroy Gardiner was born. I wanted to name him after his father, but Patrick said every man should have his own name. He's an eager young man, arriving almost three weeks early, but he is perfect, a beautiful little boy! The next one will be a girl, I know. Patrick says don't even think about another one now, but I can't help it. There have been so many wasted years already. I feel I must hurry.

Thoughtfully, Katherine put the diary away and started to dress. She had known very few women who would be eager to begin another pregnancy so soon after experiencing the painful process of bringing a child into the world. Remembering Mr.Worthingham's saying no other babies had survived, she wondered if Frances Grace had a premonition that she would never be granted that house full of children she so wanted.

The boys were almost through breakfast when they spied their grandmother in the doorway. Over their noisy greetings her son grinned at her.

"Hi sleepyhead! Is our wild social life here wearing you down? You always used to be up at the crack of dawn."

Katherine shrugged and smiled. "Age has its prerogatives and I intend to claim all of mine."

Both Fern and Mark hooted at the reference to her age.

Before they finished breakfast, Julie arrived alone. The presence of both their aunt and their grandmother, combined with the anticipation of Santa's visit had transformed two quiet little boys into bundles of noisy excitement. They threw themselves at their Aunt Julie with shouts of joy. After the greetings subsided, Mark took them outside to expend some of the excess energy playing catch.

In the quiet following their exodus, Julie reached out to hug her brother's wife. "I'm so very sorry about your accident, Fern. Are you all right now?"

Fern's eyes misted momentarily as Julie's sympathy touched her deep sorrow. She returned the embrace affectionately.

"Thanks, Julie. I'm fine."

Then the sadness vanished in amusement as the girl turned to embrace her mother.

"Mom! I honestly didn't know you for a few seconds! You look wonderful! What have you done to yourself?"

"Cut my hair and lost forty pounds," Katherine replied promptly.

The next question was a little hesitant. "Are you... is everything okay?"

"Couldn't be better, Honey." Katherine's tone was lightly evasive. "I'm working hard and enjoying it very much."

Julie studied her mother a moment as if trying to evaluate her words, then smiled. "Well, it certainly seems to agree with you."

"Julie, where's the guest you told Dad you were bringing?" Fern asked.

"I left him to help Dad build a stand for the Christmas tree while I helped you here," Julie explained.

Fern promptly pushed her chair back from the table. "In that case, let's get busy. We've got a big day ahead!"

The final decorating and gift-wrapping were interwoven with preparation of the meal planned for that evening. Favorite recipes were spiced with banter and gossip and accompanied by much laughter as they worked.

Outnumbered by the females of his family, Mark, with sons, retreated to his father's house. Fern hurriedly phoned a warning so Charles wouldn't be caught working on a Christmas tree that was still supposed to be at the North Pole. No sooner had she put the phone back in its cradle than it rang. She answered and handed the receiver to Katherine.

"It's for you."

When she heard the caller's voice Katherine exclaimed, "Dorry! It's about time you called. I've been going crazy wondering what was going on." Caught by the excitement in Katherine's voice all work stopped as her family stood listening.

"We've been too busy trying to stop what was going on," Dorry said. "Maw's boyfriend convinced her that it wasn't fair that she wasn't getting any money for my work."

"But she knew that. It was in the contract she signed."

"I know, but Jim told her she was being cheated. They came to the motel and demanded money from me. Maw said she knew I had it or I couldn't be living so high on the hog in a fancy motel. I told them I didn't have any money because you were paying my expenses.

"Then that filthy son-of-a-bitch said, 'No money, huh? Well, I'll just have to take you in the bedroom and teach you how to earn some."

"Maw said, 'The hell you will', and he said, 'The hell I won't.' He grabbed my arm and started to drag me toward the bedroom"

"Dorry! How awful! What did you do?"

"Well, the cavalry got there just in time."

"Don't be funny. What do you mean?"

"Sorry." Dorry's bravado slipped a little. "It wasn't at all funny. Paul was coming to take me to dinner and when he heard Maw's voice inside, he just opened the door and walked in. He was so furious that he scared them both. When he got through telling them what he would do if they ever bothered me again they couldn't leave fast enough."

"Oh, Dorry! I'm so glad you weren't hurt. I never dreamed you'd be in danger in the motel."

"But there's more, Katherine."

"Oh, no! What happened?"

"Maw and Jim figured if they couldn't get money out of me, they would just take some of the furniture out of the Gardiner house and sell it. They knew it was worth a lot because of all that publicity in the paper about its value when we found it. With everyone gone for the holidays it was pretty easy."

"Oh, no!" Katherine was devastated. That furniture was to have been the heart of her showplace. "What did they take?"

"They took about half of the smaller pieces. The old truck they rented wouldn't hold anymore, but it doesn't matter, Katherine."

"Dorothea!" Katherine exploded.

"I mean it doesn't matter what they took because Paul got it all back and Maw and Jim are in jail."

"Oh my gosh, why didn't you say that in the first place? I nearly had heart failure."

"Sorry, I didn't, mean to scare you. Katherine, I've got to go now. Paul is here and we have to go to the police department to file a complaint against Maw and Jim. I'll tell you everything later."

When Katherine hung up she was deluged with questions to which she had only sketchy answers. She satisfied her family's curiosity as well as she could as they finished the preparations for the Christmas Eve gathering of the family.

CHAPTER TWENTY-SIX

By the time the male members of the family returned for the evening meal, Mark and his father found themselves on excellent terms with Julie's friend, David Johnson.

David was a big blonde Swedish youth with striking blue eyes and a quiet, yet assured manner. The boys already adored him.

Sans naps, the youngsters had become very tired and dirty. Katherine volunteered to bathe them while Julie and Fern prepared the table for the evening meal. From the bathroom she could hear the talk and laughter against a background of Christmas music on the stereo. Charles' voice rose clearly over the others telling one of his favorite stories.

Suddenly, she was swept by a wave of loneliness. This was her son's home and she was only a visitor. She had no home, no place she belonged, no one to whom her presence was necessary. It wasn't until Mark touched her cheek that she became aware of the tears.

"Are you crying, Gramma?"

"I should say not!" She caught his wet hand and kissed it. "You just dripped all over me!"

This invited giggles and so much splashing that she was obliged to change her clothes after she finished dressing the boys in pajamas and robes.

During the meal, Katherine decided she liked David Johnson very much. He seemed to have made a hit with all the family and Katherine suspected he might be more than just a friend to Julie. Although her daughter had said nothing to indicate this, there was something special in her expression when their eyes met. It was as if they shared a secret no one else knew.

Engrossed in her speculations, she was surprised to discover that Ricky was sound asleep in his high chair and Mark was struggling to stay awake long enough to finish his dessert. He was too tired to object when his dad scooped him up to carry him to bed. All he asked for was reassurance that Santa would really come in the night and leave a tree and presents. Julie smilingly followed with Ricky.

When it was considered safe to do so, Charles brought in the tree. It was a big one which was placed in front of the picture window and the decorating party began. It didn't take long with so many helping hands. Julie was granted the honor of performing the final touch; crowning its topmost branch with a golden star. The lights were turned on and everyone stood back to admire their handiwork.

"I think it's the most beautiful tree we've ever had," Julie asserted.

Her brother laughed. "You say that every year, Sis."

"She does," Charles agreed, "but it's probably true. Think of all the years of practice we've had."

Everyone now began to retrieve packages from various hiding places. The accumulation soon covered most of the cotton snowfield under the tree and had to be stacked against the wall on each side. Finally Mark went out to the garage for the one gift Mark, Jr. had asked for all year; a puppy. He took the little wriggly ball of fur out of its carrying crate to be fondled and petted while the crate was appropriately decorated. When it was finished, it was placed conspicuously under the tree. The pup was returned to a temporary pen in the garage for the night and the party broke up.

In the holiday gaiety, no one had acknowledged the almost imperceptible air of strain between Katherine and Charles. Katherine carefully maintained her appearance of unruffled indifference, but she resented his presence and he knew it.

"I suppose he'll be back bright and early in the morning," she said sourly as they watched his car back out of the driveway. " He certainly isn't spending much time with that precious dream girl he can't live without!"

Fern looked surprised. "She's not here. I thought Charles would have told you. She went to Illinois to spend Christmas with her family."

"No, he didn't mention it." Katherine sounded angry. "I believe he's aware that she isn't my favorite topic of conversation," she added spitefully.

"Probably," Fern agreed in a neutral tone, as she turned away. "I think I'll go to bed. I'm tired and the kids will be up at the crack of dawn."

She was right, of course. It was barely daylight when Katherine, who had spent a restless night, heard a thud from the boys' room. Ricky had half fallen out of his crib in his hurry to follow Mark into the hall. They had strict orders not to touch anything under the tree until everyone was up and Mark spoke quickly when he saw his grandmother in the doorway.

"I didn't touch anything, honest Gramma."

Katherine knelt to hug him. "I know that, Honey, but it's hard isn't it?"

Ricky toddled up and she included him in the hug. "Listen, you take your little brother in the kitchen and I'll come and fix you some breakfast as soon as I get my robe."

Fern poked her head out of her bedroom. "I'll do that if you'll see that the garage door is closed." She winked at Katherine.

"Oh, sure thing." Katherine got her robe and then proceeded to smuggle the puppy into his carrying crate under the tree while their mother held the boys' attention.

They were almost through with breakfast when Julie called to ask if her nephews were up yet.

Assured they were, she chuckled, "I knew they would be. We'll be there in ten minutes."

Fern was just lifting Ricky down from his high chair when the doorbell rang and the puppy barked.

"A puppy!" Mark screeched with Ricky echoing him as they ran for the living room, nearly tripping their dad as he went to open the front door.

Katherine followed slowly. She had not slept well. Trying to maintain an air of serenity was a strain with the constant irritation of Charles' presence. She had not expected him to be hanging around all the time when she decided to stay through the holidays and it was annoying. It's not that I'm letting Charles bother me, she thought, unaware of how many times she had denied her ex-husband's influence lately. I couldn't care less what he does. I'm just tired of marking time here. Forcing her brightest smile, she joined the merriment around the Christmas tree, hoping no one would notice her heart was not in it.

The day after Christmas found Katherine alone in an unusually quiet house. Mark and Fern, with the children, were paying holiday visits to their friends. Katherine had excused herself from the expedition, pleading fatigue. She was not really tired, but restless and worried. There still had been no further word from Paul or Dorothea. She considered canceling her January second reservation and taking an earlier plane back to Maryland. A brief calculation of the chances of finding an empty seat at this season put an end to that line of thought. Anyway, if there was anything else drastically wrong, Paul was probably more capable of handling it than she would be. Besides it was only a few days more.

According to Dorothea's last letter, the water line work had been completed and Lily and Fred were back in their apartment. The bathrooms in the house were not yet entirely finished so there was still no water there. Going back early would just mean waiting in the motel room instead of waiting here.

Katherine tried to read, but nothing held her interest. She sorted her clothing and put a few things in the suitcase, but it was too soon for any serious packing. She was beginning to regret her decision to stay home when the telephone broke into her growing frustration. It was Julie.

"Mom, David and I have to leave tomorrow morning because he has to be back to work the next day. I would like to take you to lunch; just you and me, so we could have a little private girl talk before I leave. Is it okay if I pick you up in about twenty minutes?"

Katherine agreed with pleasure. She was pretty sure that the subject of the 'girl talk' probably would be David. Her daughter's manner strongly suggested that the young man had been presented for the family's approval and Julie was now ready to announce what everyone had already guessed.

Julie had more to confide than her mother had anticipated. Not only was she engaged, she had moved into David's apartment. They would marry next year.

"Mom, you remember when we had that talk about sex . . . the time we both got so angry?"

Wondering what new shock was coming, Katherine nodded.

"I remember."

"Mom," Julie's eyes were shining with intense emotion, "I know now what you were trying to tell me. Really loving someone makes it so different. I don't know why, but it just isn't the same. Its almost," she paused as if afraid of sounding maudlin, "it's as if we were part of each other."

Her mother reached across the table and clasped her hand tightly.

"What else? It's the act that joins two people together to create life, Honey. I'm glad you feel that way."

"But, Mom, I don't regret the other experiences. I wouldn't know the difference, otherwise, and I still don't think it was wrong."

Katherine smiled wryly, thinking of her disastrous evening with Paul.

"We won't talk about that, Julie. We each have to satisfy our own conscience. I'm just happy that you're happy."

Julie's bliss welled up and she spent the rest of the lunch describing the wonders of David. While Katherine was quite impressed with her daughter's choice, she wasn't sorry when the non-stop recital of his perfection finally came to an end and Julie drove her home.

That evening David and Julie came by to make the official announcement of their engagement and to say goodbye to everyone. Julie was now wearing a modest engagement ring and an aura of radiance. Katherine could not help wishing the wedding could have come before the honeymoon, but it was impossible not to be glad for their glowing happiness.

Charles was there, too. For the moment he was only Julie's father in Katherine's mind.

"Do you think it will work out?" she asked hopefully.

"I think so." Charles' tone was thoughtful. "He seems to be a very stable person and he's certainly deeply in love with Julie."

Involuntarily Katherine glanced up at Charles. You were deeply in love with me once, she told herself. With that thought, Charles was again a source of resentment. It hung in the air between them for a moment, then Katherine lowered her gaze and picked up the coffee pot to refill her cup.

"Katherine," he said hesitantly, but she turned her back and walked away across the room.

The next morning Katherine awoke with a scratchy throat and a thick feeling in her head. "Oh damn!" she groaned. "All I need is a miserable cold!"

She plodded down to the kitchen, took two aspirins and returned to bed fortified with a box of cough drops and a cup of steaming lemon tea. She was dozing lightly and opened her eyes when Fern looked in on her.

"Sorry, I didn't mean to disturb you, but you're usually up before I am. Are you all right?"

"You didn't disturb me. I think I'm getting a cold and a little extra rest seemed like a good idea."

"I'm sorry, but I'm not surprised. Both of the boys have the sniffles this morning."

Katherine and her grandsons all developed matching red noses. Their eyes watered and they disposed of mounds of tissues, but Mark and Fern seemed immune. None of the sufferers was very ill and Katherine spent a couple of days keeping the boys quietly entertained. She even regarded the indisposition as having a good

side. Fern had been urging her to go to a New Year's Eve party she
had no desire to attend. Now she could gracefully excuse herself from
the party and also retire to her room if Charles dropped in again.

Charles did not put in an appearance, however. When Fern
casually mentioned having seen Betty in the shopping mall, Katherine
was assailed by an abrupt stab of animosity. It wasn't jealousy she
assured herself, just resentment that the other woman had
coldheartedly snatched something Katherine considered hers.

On the last day of December Katherine sat in the yard soaking
up the California sun and watching her grandsons play with the
puppy. She had just finished reading the last letter from Paul. There
had been several letters from him, informal progress reports, but
nothing personal. She knew she had destroyed the chance of
developing anything personal with Paul and except for the momentary
embarrassment, that didn't bother her. She felt only relief that their
relationship seemed to have returned to a friendly business alliance.
Apparently he was keeping his promise to look after Dorothea
because her letters mentioned him frequently.

Her thoughts were interrupted by Ricky's giggles as he rolled
on the grass and the puppy tried to lick his face. Then the pup
suddenly darted over to where Katherine sat on the porch steps and
started chewing on some tender grass shoots.

"Look." She pointed as Mark followed the pup. "He's eating
his spinach."

Mark shook his head. "No, it's milk."

His grandmother looked puzzled. "But that's green. Milk is
white."

"Cows eat grass and it turns to milk," Mark insisted. "It gets
that way when the sun shines a lot."

Katherine's laughter brought Fern out of the house to sit beside her in the sun. She tried again to interest Katherine in the New Year's Eve party. "I'll feel guilty about leaving you here alone while we're out having a good time."

"I won't be alone. I'll have my two favorite boyfriends and that killer guard dog over there."

Fern laughed. "Okay, if that's the way you want it. After all, I don't often get a free baby-sitter."

CHAPTER TWENTY-SEVEN

Their mother insisted on seeing the boys bathed and tucked in bed before she dressed for the party, so there was little for Katherine to do when she was left alone. The house seemed awfully quiet. She turned on the television for a while, but it was boring. She snapped it off and went to take her bath, soaking leisurely until the water began to cool.

Pulling her nightgown from the drawer flipped the red diary out on the floor. Now too wide-awake for bed, Katherine put on a robe and curled up on the couch to read. The farther she went in the book, the harder it was to decipher. The pages had evidently become wet and a large number were welded together. Trying to separate them only resulted in tearing the fragile paper. Eventually, she gave up on this part and skipped to the few undamaged pages near the back of the book.

At first she thought these pages had been written by someone else, but finally concluded the book had been abandoned for another long period of years. Frances Grace had apparently resumed confiding in the diary when her husband died. Many missing years appeared to have been in the ruined part.

Where it became legible again, she was no longer dating her entries. Sometimes she seemed to ramble. Without dates, Katherine could only guess at her age. While she sometimes seemed confused about time, her love for Patrick and her thwarted dreams of children's voices resounding through her house remained bright and clear. She wrote as if she were talking directly to Patrick.

Patrick, do you remember when Albert married Jennifer? He got so angry because you suggested he should settle down and take over the estate. He said he'd never live in this inconvenient old barn. Well, he's living here now. He's broke again and wants me to sell the property but I have nowhere else to go. He threatened to sell all the lovely furniture we had made just for this house, but I couldn't let that happen. I had a moving company put it in the secret room where they used to hide the slaves escaping on the underground railway. I was afraid he might remember the room but he didn't or else he never thought of my hiding the furniture. When I told him I sold it to pay my debts, he was so furious I was a little frightened, but it must stay with the house. Someday there will be children here, I know it.

I saw Mr. Worthingham today, Patrick. I couldn't help telling him a little of my concern for our home. He has promised that he will try to find a family with children to buy it if Albert does not want to live here after I'm gone.

Many of the entries were references Katherine did not understand, as they were about the past. Many of them twisted Katherine's heart with their loneliness.

My Dear, I do not feel well today. I miss you so. I know it is wrong, but I can't help wishing for the day when we will be together again. Perhaps it is only the rain that is making me so gloomy. This morning I noticed two damp spots on the ceiling of the master bedroom. When I went up into the attic I found a tiny trickle of water running down the chimney. I will have to find someone to fix it because Albert refuses to do anything. He said it was too small a leak to worry about and the old house isn't worth fixing anyway. I know that isn't true, Patrick, but I can feel sadness in its neglected walls. Sometimes I even hear the cries of our lost babies when the wind blows.

There was only one more entry in the diary.

I feel much worse today, Patrick. Albert went for the doctor and he has been gone so long that the fire has burned down. The room is very cold. I think I will soon be with you again, my Dear, and I am glad.

Katherine closed the book with a deep feeling of sadness. Then she quickly opened it again as she realized the significance of the next to last entry. The roof was good, she had had it checked. The problem must be in the chimney. Now she knew why her plaster had failed to harden, and she knew no ghost had killed Albert. He was responsible for his own death trap. That thick old plaster had been rock hard when the leak had loosened it and sent it crashing down on his head.

Katherine wished she had not chosen this particular night to finish the diary. She identified too closely with the aching loneliness of that old house. Charles wasn't dead, but her marriage was. It had died long before his betrayal of their wedding vows. Neglect had killed it. The last thing she wanted was to go back to that unhappy relationship, yet she wondered if she could ever build new emotional ties to someone else.

A couple of sneezes sent her into the kitchen for another hot lemon drink. This one she impulsively laced with bourbon.

"After all," she told her reflection in the kitchen windowpane, "it's New Year's Eve!"

Back in the front room, she switched on the TV and sat watching as the program host visited various parties and introduced the celebrities. It was just a quarter of twelve when she was startled

by the doorbell. The little peephole revealed a distorted view of
Charles' face and she swung the door open.

"What are you doing here?"

"I just came by to see how you are," he said defensively.
"Fern said you were ill. Sorry I bothered you."

"It's all right," she said reluctantly. "I just have a cold. I'm
sorry I snapped at you, but you scared me. After all, it is the middle of
the night."

"I know." He grinned and held up a bottle of champagne. "I
thought we might have a little drink to welcome the New Year."

For a moment, Katherine was at a loss. Then she realized that
Charles, nearly a teetotaler, had already had several drinks. While he
wasn't drunk, he was as eagerly friendly as the new Christmas puppy
that was now asleep on the foot of Mark's bed. She couldn't help
laughing.

"I suppose we might. Come on in."

Katherine brought two glasses and Charles ceremoniously
opened and poured the bubbly wine to the first strains of 'Ould Lang
Syne' They sat quietly sipping their drinks, watching the celebrants
on TV and making polite formal conversation.

This is the most peculiar New Year's party I've ever attended,
Katherine thought. She wondered why Charles was here and where
Betty was, but with the champagne resting on top of the bourbon it
really didn't matter. Nothing mattered very much and she felt fine.

Gradually, their desultory comments ran out and Charles rose
to leave.

"Well," he said rather lamely, "Happy New Year, Katy."

She had also risen politely. "Thank you. Happy New Year to
you, too."

There was an awkward pause and it dawned on Katherine that he wanted to kiss her goodnight and was afraid to try. It was so outrageous that she was caught between the desire to kill him or laugh at him. Laughter won. That obviously offended Charles. Resentfully, he grasped her shoulders and kissed her roughly.

The touch of his lips was like an unexpected jolt of electricity that made Katherine's heart jump wildly. Already a little unsteady from the alcohol, she lost her balance and would have fallen if he had not caught her against his body. Katherine could not believe what she was feeling. She had always reacted with normal enjoyment to appropriate sexual stimulation. Never, however, had she been stormed by the fiery lust that suddenly flared through every part of her body. She saw surprise, then delight in his eyes as Charles became conscious of her response.

His mouth found her's eagerly and his tongue tasted deeply while caressing hands explored her body. With one hand he untied her robe and gently massaged the taut nipple that rose against the silky gown.

Even through the sheet of flame enveloping her, Katherine was aware of an analytical part of her mind telling her Charles' technique had improved. That part also told her that she had drunk too much champagne, but she didn't care. Her deepest primitive urges were in total control. The sensations elicited by Charles' hands and mouth left no room for other reactions.

A slight noise made them aware of the children and Charles walked her backward into her bedroom, unwilling to let her go, even for a moment. They undressed in the dark and came together eagerly on her bed. His mouth sought first one still firm breast, then the other, and his feathery touch inspired growing desire. Katherine's urgency became frantic. When Charles entered her, her gasp was part pain, part pleasure. He stopped in concern.

"Am I hurting you?"

"Only a little, it's been a long time."

He began to move, slowly at first, then more rapidly and Katherine matched each move with mounting pleasure until the summit engulfed her in a glorious explosion that was like drowning in pure physical sensation.

Charles fell back on his pillow with a sigh that was half groan. "Oh Katy, Katy, Katy!" Then there was an almost stunned silence as their breathing returned to normal. Presently he got up and began to dress without turning on the light. Katherine didn't move. Her thoughts were in absolute chaos as she lay watching his shadowy movements.

His voice was subdued as he turned to the door. "Come into the front room, Katy. We've got to talk."

CHAPTER TWENTY-EIGHT

Katherine and Charles had no chance to talk privately before she left for Maryland. Just as she entered the living room the front door opened to admit Fern and Mark. They stopped in surprise at finding Charles there. Smothering her curiosity, Fern invited him to stay for a midnight supper.

Awakened by unguarded voices and laughter, the boys wandered sleepily into the kitchen. Delighted by the novelty of a meal in the middle of the night, they demanded their share of the scrambled eggs as well as their grandparent's attention.

Charles appeared upset and impatient at being unable to talk to her and soon left. Unable to explain his visit because she didn't understand it herself, Katherine told her son and daughter-in-law a quick goodnight and escaped to her room.

She was distracted and ardently desired a period of solitude to assess what had happened to her. She thought Charles seemed to be ashamed of his behavior and she could only feel amazement at her own heedless response. Never in her life had she so abandoned all restraint. Probably the champagne was partly responsible, but she was sure there was more to it than that.

In spite of her disordered thoughts, her body gratefully accepted the release of physical tension and she slept through what was left of the night.

Katherine's direct flight was scheduled for noon. All morning she half-expected Charles to call, but he didn't. Fern betrayed a lively curiosity about her father-in-law's visit but Katherine's attitude discouraged personal questions.

"Will you be coming back soon?" she asked cautiously.

"No," Katherine answered slowly, "I don't think so. I believe my future is in Maryland."

She boarded her plane deeply perplexed. Between restless naps, she found herself questioning last night from every angle. She could not really believe she had been deliberately seduced. Charles simply wasn't that kind of a person, yet, a year ago she would not have believed he could be an unfaithful husband either.

It seemed humiliatingly probable that she had simply made an ass of herself and he had responded as any normal male would.

However, even as Katherine struggled with a sense of mortification, recollection of that flaming sensation surging through her body made her uncomfortably warm. She was shocked and embarrassed. How could she react this way to dull, unexciting, cheating Charles?

Now that she thought about it, if he was so dull and unexciting why had she enjoyed his companionship on that shopping trip? Why had his touch ignited a fire that she had been convinced was long dead? Ruefully, she concluded that there was probably a lot of truth in the old adage that you often fail to recognize the value of something until you lose it.

Yet, even with the recognition that there was still a strong sexual attraction between them, Katherine didn't think she would want him back if she could have him. She had changed so much since the bombshell of Betty had blasted her life, she could never go back to the old apathy and boredom.

She wanted to believe Charles had taken advantage of her, but she kept remembering his surprise at her response when he had kissed her. What had made her do that? Was it the mixture of bourbon and champagne? How could she have forgotten, even for a moment, that he had dumped her for another woman. She could find no answers acceptable to her pride. Apparently her hormones could still make a fool of her, even at her age.

Her speculations ended with a final impasse. Charles had made a commitment to someone else. Nothing that had happened really changed that. She was glad when the 'Fasten your seat belt' sign put an end to her unwelcome thoughts.

To Katherine's surprise, Paul was with Dorothea at the terminal. Her young friend greeted her with an enthusiastic hug.

"Gosh, I've missed you!"

"Well, I worried about you, but I can see Paul has been taking good care of you."

He laughed and kissed her on the cheek in a very brotherly manner. "It's good to have you back, Katy. How was your visit?"

"Everything considered, it was a good visit. My daughter-in-law is recovering rapidly and we had a very nice Christmas." Her manner was a little formal as she busily fished in her purse for the baggage checks.

"That's good." Paul reached for the checks. "Let me have those. After we get your bags, we'll go have a bite to eat. You are hungry, aren't you?"

All at once Katherine's stomach remembered she had refused the meals offered on the plane. She really was hungry.

"I could eat," she said, winking at Dorothea, "but the real reason I want to go to dinner, is because I can see that Dorry is starving to death!"

Her helper laughed at Katherine. "I didn't know it showed, but you're right. Paul wouldn't feed me until you got here."

Paul obviously liked her teasing. He looked at Katy and shrugged. "She's always hungry. I suppose she'll be going on a diet next month."

After the past weeks of worrying about possible constraint in working with Paul, Katherine was relieved at his easy friendly manner. Her slight reserve vanished in her eager questions about the furniture.

"How did you find out it had been stolen?"

"It was Lily who found the house had been broken into," Dorry said. "She had been checking on it every day. She called me and I called Paul and the police."

"It was a good thing she discovered it immediately," Paul said gratefully. "If we hadn't found out for a week or two they would have sold it in Baltimore and we'd never have found it all again."

"How did you get it back?"

Dorry started laughing. "They might have gotten away with it, but they were sticking to all the back roads and their old junky truck broke down. It was the middle of the night and they had to walk several miles to find a phone. It was daylight by the time they got a garage to send out a tow truck."

"The tow truck driver said the people were acting so nervous," Paul cut in, "that he got suspicious. He thought they might be carrying dope or something. He called his dispatcher and she told him the boss said to haul the truck to the police station and let them check it out."

"I wish I'd been there," Dorry chimed in. "When they stepped out of that truck they were surrounded by a ring of police with drawn guns."

"Still," Paul said when they quit laughing, "we were lucky. The police didn't know about the furniture theft yet and were about to let them go, but Dorothea's stepmother went to pieces. She accused Jim of talking her into it and then, of course, he claimed it was all her idea. By the time the police realized they were dealing with a theft, the police bulletin came in on the computer and both of them were arrested."

CHAPTER TWENTY-NINE

It was late when Paul finally left them at the little motel after dinner. The day had been so long and thought provoking, Katherine felt as if she had boarded that plane a week ago, but now her problems were mostly personal. It was surprising how much more professional her restoration project appeared as she realized what competent people she was working with. Dorothea wasn't just 'the hired girl'; she was a very responsible young woman who could be depended on in her boss' absence. Paul may have been looking out for his own interests, but that meant protecting her's too. The thought was so comforting that Katherine relaxed into a dreamless sleep within minutes of closing her eyes.

Dorothea was up early and had breakfast ready by the time Katherine was awake. They had barely finished eating when the phone rang. It was Paul.

"Don't bother unpacking your bags," he told Katherine. "The plumber just called to tell me the bathrooms are finished and the water was turned on this morning. You can move back in."

Katherine could not have asked for anything more satisfactory and felt an irrational sense of gratitude to the spirit of Frances Grace for quickly drawing her into the vortex of work again. Keeping busy was a welcome refuge from her personal problems.

Dorothea packed her things in short order and they each made several passes through the motel apartment to be sure nothing had been overlooked. Katherine settled their bill while Dorry started the car and warmed the engine.

"Would you like me to drive?" she asked hopefully when Katherine returned.

Although Dorothea was a good driver, she had seldom had a car at her disposal before and she loved driving

"Sure, go ahead," Katherine smiled and went around to slide into the passenger seat.

It was a bright clear day but the air was icy and there was no warmth to the sun. There were patches of old snow in shady spots. Although the road was clear, several small bridges were still slick with remaining ice. When they came to a stop in the driveway, Katherine opened the car door to a blast of cold wind that made her draw her coat tightly around her. It was a shocking change from the California climate, but she instantly forgot it in her surge of pride as she looked up at the sparkling white walls accented with clean blue trim.

Inside, it was warmer only by comparison as the heat control had been set just high enough to prevent freezing. The new plaster still smelled and their footsteps were loud as they carried their belongings upstairs. Katherine turned up the thermostat in passing, but they kept their coats on as they went from room to room, eagerly inspecting the new bathrooms.

Katherine knew she had done well. Paul's architect had made only one change in her sketches. The wall dimensions and color schemes had been followed faithfully and each new bathroom nestled into place like part of the original room. By the time they had tried all the taps and flushed all the toilets, the house had become comfortably warm. Katherine again felt that same glow of pride at having melded a bit of history with the comfort of the present century.

Downstairs Lily and Fred had just arrived wearing broad smiles of welcome. Fred started a fire in the big stove and Lily began checking the kitchen supplies and listing her needs.

"It's sure nice to have you all back," she told Katherine in her soft drawl. "That Fred over there was gettin' downright lazy with no chores to do."

Fred just grinned at her sally. "Gimme that list woman, if you want those groceries in time for lunch."

When he was gone, Lily led Katherine and Dorothea into the pantry where she had filled almost all the available space with rows of carefully taped and wrapped drapes.

"I didn't know where they go," she told Katherine, "so I just put'em all in here."

Katherine gazed at the lengths of plastic wrapped material.

"I've almost forgotten where they go, myself," she said in a slightly awed tone. "Guess I'd better get out my work sheets." She turned to leave and then came back to look again. "I wonder if they could have made a mistake. That looks like enough drapes for two houses."

She had just found the work sheets in her desk when the phone rang. Paul wanted to know if she was ready for the carpets to be installed.

"Sure thing," she told him. "They can come anytime."

"How do you like the bathrooms?"

"They're beautiful!" she assured him. "Not a single mistake. You must have hired some pretty good contractors."

"You can thank your 'straw boss' for that," he said. "Dorothea was right on their tails every minute. She didn't want them to change a wall or even a piece of tile from the way you had planned it. She fought with the architect when he tried to move one of the walls and the plumber had to appeal to me when the fixtures didn't match the pipes in one bathroom." He was laughing, but there was admiration underlining his amusement.

"Well, I'm certainly glad she was here, then," Katherine said in some surprise, "but she hasn't said one word about any problems. I didn't even know she was here while the work was being done."

"Never missed a day," he chuckled. "She saw to it that there weren't any problems. She's one very special young woman, Katy."

Thoughtfully, Katherine hung up the phone. She wondered if it was her imagination that there had been a suggestion of personal interest in Paul's voice. As quickly as the thought came she dismissed it. Paul was old enough to be Dorothea's father and much too sophisticated to be intrigued by such an inexperienced young woman. Nevertheless, perhaps it was as well she was back to keep an eye on things.

To Katherine, labor was the antidote to worry. She threw herself into her work determined not to think about her personal problems. Being tired made it easier to sleep nights

She hired a bricklayer to find and repair the hidden leak in the chimney.

Carpets were laid in the bedrooms, but Katherine insisted on refinishing and polishing the huge salon floor before covering it with area rugs. Frances Grace had said there would be children in this house one day. The logical extension of that vision was parties and dances.

The dining room chairs came back with beautiful new damask seats closely resembling the old ones. When another hand was needed, Fred installed the hardware and Lily helped to hang the drapes. This made Katherine realize Kenney had not been around since her return, but she forgot to ask about him.

When the drapes were up, Paul listed the house for sale. Katherine objected mildly because the kitchen was not finished. Paul argued that since this was such a special house it would take time to find the right buyer and they should start early.

"Well," she conceded, "you should know, that's your business, but I would think most women would consider the kitchen of first importance."

"Possibly," he agreed good-naturedly, "but I suspect the woman of this house will probably be in a position to depend on hired help in her kitchen. Besides, I expect you will have it finished by the time we get a serious buyer."

Katherine knew she was being humored, but she just laughed. Her relationship with Paul no longer carried the original spark of excitement, but he was a friend she trusted even though they didn't always agree

The kitchen range turned out to be one of the things they didn't agree about. He thought she was crazy to keep it as a centerpiece of the old-fashioned kitchen. All the modern appliances were disguised as matching cabinets. Even the electric stove was hidden under a folding counter top. It looked like a farm kitchen of a hundred years ago with copper pans hanging above the range and a wooden table and chairs in the center of the room.

The first clients to view the finished project finally won his grudging admission that it might have been a good idea, after all. He couldn't help being impressed by the lady's extravagant praise of the unusual decor. Lily, who had wholeheartedly agreed with Paul, sniffed disdainfully after the couple left.

"If she had to cook on that stove all the time, she wouldn't think it was so wonderful!"

"I know," Katherine chortled gleefully, "but that's the beauty of it. It's fantastic as a decorator piece, but if it's ever needed it could be mighty practical, too."

Lily, who had spent a number of hours with stove blacking and polish, clearly remained unconvinced.

"I guess it does look like a picture in a magazine," she admitted, "but kitchens have come a long way since those days."

Dorothea came back from seeing Paul and his clients to the car.

"I think Paul wasted his time bringing that pair out here," she announced. "She spent more time ogling Paul than she did looking at the house."

Noting the adult female quality of that observation, Katherine again became aware of Dorry's maturity. It was easy to believe Paul's claim that she had been a capable 'straw boss' in Katherine's absence. Her girlish looks were deceiving.

"Dorry," she asked on impulse, "don't you have a birthday coming up soon?"

"That's right," Dorry nodded. "I thought I would be twenty-one in two weeks, but when I applied for a copy of my birth certificate I found Maw lied about my age when I was eighteen so she could keep on getting child support. I'll really be twenty- three and I was going to start hinting pretty soon if nobody remembered," she added.

"Oh you were! And just what kind of a celebration did you have in mind?"

Dorothea drew a deep breath and looked very serious. "Do you think we could have a formal dinner here, evening gowns and cocktails and champagne? Not a birthday party with gifts or anything like that, that's for kids. I've never been to a glamorous dinner party like that and this is such a perfect place for it."

"I think that would be fantastic! But whom would you like to invite? We don't know very many people around here."

"You and Paul, of course, and Mr. Worthingham. I talked to him on the phone at Christmas time and he said he would like very much to see what you have done to the house. And Mr. Minyard and his wife. He told Paul he'd like to see where so much of the bank's money has gone."

She stopped and Katherine asked, "And Kenney?"

Dorry shook her head. "No, I would rather not. He was getting serious and it didn't seem fair to let him think I cared in the same way, so I don't see him anymore."

Katherine thought about the guests the girl had named, all older people with an interest in the house.

"This isn't really a birthday party you want, is it Dorry?"

"No," she admitted soberly. "Living here and working with you has been the happiest time I've ever known in my life. That will all end when the house is sold. My stepmother is in jail. I wouldn't go back to her anyway, and Virginia and the baby are in a foster home where they are much better cared for now. I don't know where my next job will be. I just thought my birthday might be an excuse for a farewell party."

A farewell party! The words were a shock to Katherine. She hadn't thought much about what would happen after she reached her ultimate goal of a successful restoration and sale of the property. Clearly Dorothea had. In that moment Katherine felt a sharp reluctance to relinquish control of her achievement to some unknown who might not appreciate it. It was like sending a child off to school for the first time.

Dorry had been waiting for her reaction and now she asked, "Do you mind? Would you rather not have that kind of a party?"

"I'm not sure it would be appropriate as a birthday party, Dorry. Would you mind if we honor your birthday in private, with gifts," she emphasized with a smile, "and plan a formal farewell party to celebrate when we finish the house?"

"Of course I wouldn't mind," Dorry exulted. "That's a better plan than mine, especially the gift part," she joked. "I'd love it!"

When Paul came back that evening, he thought it was a good plan too, and immediately set about changing it. He proposed adding carefully selected prospective buyers to the guest list for the formal dinner. Katherine would rather have kept the occasion small and personal but she was forced to admit that it would be an excellent promotion scheme. Dorothea was infected by Paul's enthusiasm and hugely flattered at being credited with a clever business idea. She sparkled under his praise.

Katherine was a bit taken back to realize she had been forgotten in their eager planning. She was struck by the recognition of an intellectual accord between them that transcended the difference in their ages. Paul was the eternal Peter Pan while Dorothea was far more mature than her years. Occasionally his glance at her held surprise and something else that was definitely not avuncular.

When she saw Paul's birthday gift to Dorothea, a stunning necklace of matched pearls, Katherine knew his interest was not casual, whatever he might have in mind.

Paul insisted on taking them to the Holly Inn to celebrate the occasion. Dorothea wore a strikingly simple green wool dress that made her look like a fashion model. Heads turned as they walked into the dining room. He had made arrangements ahead for her to be presented with a decorated cake topped with twenty-three candles, but he was a little surprised when the waitresses gathered at their table to sing Happy Birthday. Many of the diners around them joined in. Dorry's face was scarlet at being the center of attention and her eyes glistened.

"Hey, wait a minute," Paul exclaimed. "I didn't mean to make you cry."

"Tears of happiness, Paul," Dorothea said, dabbing at her eyes with her napkin. "Nobody ever cared about my birthday before."

Katherine was struck by Dorothea's sense of values. The expensive string of pearls was simply a lovely necklace, but a gesture of caring went to her heart.

"Well, I'll guarantee you'll never be able to make that claim again," Paul stated rather forcefully, "will she Katy?"

"No, I don't think so."

Watching their absorption in each other Katherine felt his statement was more accurate than he realized. Incredible as it seemed, she was beginning to believe the confirmed bachelor was unwittingly approaching 'parson's mousetrap' with her hard-working assistant.

As the days passed, however, Dorry gave little indication that she was taking him seriously. Katherine took a great deal of pleasure in watching the young woman's adroit handling of the situation as Paul put considerable effort into pleasing her. There was little doubt as to who was in control.

CHAPTER THIRTY

Katherine held off setting a date for the dinner party until she finished one last project. She wanted to make a game and recreation area suitable for children in the secret room.

"For the love of Pete, Katy," Paul protested, "you can't know if the buyer will even have children! He might want to make an office or something back there."

"Perhaps so," she agreed quietly, "but until you sell it, it's still my house and that's what I want."

He capitulated in obvious annoyance. "Okay, but you're getting to be pretty one-way these days, Katy."

"I have my reasons," she retorted shortly.

The next day, she set about transforming the long dark room by requesting the electrician to install a row of lights the length of the ceiling. She and Dorry then painted the ceiling a lovely sky blue and papered the walls with country scenes which included barns and farm animals in the distance.

"Well, it certainly will appeal to kids now," her helper observed as they finished pasting wallpaper, "but I wonder what it was originally intended for. It is such a strange room hidden away back here."

"It was once a station on the underground railway for escaping slaves," Katherine informed her.

"I'll be darned! How do you know that?"

"I read it in some of the old papers," Katherine said evasively.

"It's such an unusual house," Dorry said. "Paul thinks it will sell very quickly."

"I know. I hope he's right because it has been awfully expensive and it's going to take a lot of money to pay the people I owe, including you."

"Will you go back to California after it's sold?"

"I don't think so, at least not right away. There are too many painful associations."

"I'm sorry," Dorothea said. "When you stayed in California so long I thought you might have worked things out with your husband."

"No, nothing like that. I stayed at first because they needed me, and then because my son and his family wanted me to spend the holidays with them. There was really nothing I could do here until the plumbing work was finished and they knew it, so I couldn't say no."

"I wondered," Dorry was very hesitant. "For a while I thought there might be a thing between you and Paul."

Katherine laughed ruefully. "So did I, for a while. But I was married too long, I guess. I still haven't adjusted to being single yet."

"I'm sorry, but I'm glad too," Dorothea said candidly. "I think I may marry Paul."

"Dorothea!" Katherine was genuinely shocked. She had been amused at Paul's subjugation without recognizing that the young woman was equally entranced by his charm.

"Do you realize how much older he is?"

"Only in years," was the serenely accurate answer.

"Has he suggested marriage?"

"Not yet," the girl said confidently, "but he will."

Katherine, recalling Paul's recent behavior thought she was probably right. May - December marriages were not so terribly uncommon, she knew, and some of them were quite successful. Dorothea was such an unusual person the relationship was likely to go exactly as she wanted it to, and Paul would always think it was all his idea.

The dinner party was finally set for the week following Dorothea's birthday. Paul brought someone out to view the house nearly every day. More often than not, it was Dorothea who accompanied the tour, becoming more professional and poised with each experience. Katherine marveled as the blossoming May - December romance seemed to diminish the years between them. She had to admit they were truly compatible.

Katherine felt increasingly alone, not because she cared for Paul, but because their absorption in each other shut her out of their particular world. They didn't ignore her but no amount of courtesy could disguise the fact that her presence was not essential to their happiness.

She identified even more closely with the house into which she had poured so much of herself. She began to worry about her indebtedness. There was also the fear that they might never find the right buyer; the one who would fill the home with the children Frances Grace had dreamed of.

Three days before the party, Katherine startled an attractive woman who had been left behind in the library by one of the touring groups. She sat before the fire in the little rocking chair, a black curly head bent over a nursing infant.

"I hope you don't mind," she smiled, turning brilliant blue eyes up to Katherine. "It's the baby's lunch time."

"Of course not," Katherine assured her warmly. "Are you interested in buying the house?"

"Very much," the lady answered. "We have a large family so we need lots of room. From what I've seen so far, this place seems perfect and it's really beautiful."

"How many children do you have?" Katherine asked.

The mother looked down at the tiny bundle in her arms.

"Patrick here makes eight," she smiled.

"Patrick?" Katherine repeated sharply.

The matron, who appeared too youthful to have eight children, raised those incredibly blue eyes. "Don't you like that name?" she asked mildly.

"I love it!" Katherine replied emphatically. "It's the perfect name!"

Before she could ask any more questions, Paul came back to inform the lady her party was ready to leave. After he had shepherded his group out she asked Dorothea who the woman was.

"The one with the baby? Oh, her husband is the new senator. Paul doesn't think he's seriously interested. It's too far from the capitol. We don't even have him on the party list."

"Well you just better put him on the party list! Its only twenty minutes to Washington by that new commuter train. His wife is very seriously interested, and she just suits Frances Grace!"

"All right! All right!" Dorry was laughing at her vehemence. "But who is Frances Grace?"

"Just someone who used to live around here," Katherine said a bit smugly. No matter what Paul or Dorry thought, she knew a new era was beginning in this old house. It would again shelter a happy family and record important history within its sturdy walls.

On the morning of the promotion dinner, to Paul's surprise, the newly elected senator appeared in his office without an appointment. He agreed to the sale terms without argument and the preliminary papers were signed in the afternoon. Paul said it was the easiest sale he had ever made and Katherine secretly said, "Thank you, Frances Grace."

That made the party truly the farewell party Dorry had asked for. By this time the guest list had grown so large that the dinner was arranged buffet style. A number of tables had to be provided for those who couldn't be seated at the dining table. They were set with glittering silver and glassware provided by the caterer Paul had engaged.

Pausing on the curving staircase, Katherine drew a deep breath of satisfaction at the scene below. This was what this house was meant for. Once again history would be made under this roof. Instead of ghosts, the voices of real children would echo from its walls. The dreams of Frances Grace and all those who came before her would live on in its shelter.

Mr. Worthingham was the last arrival and he was late. Concerned lest the dinner should be spoiled, Katherine ordered the food put out on the long sideboard. Just as the chef was beginning to carve a huge glazed ham, her last guest came into the front entryway and he was not alone. With a sense of shock, Katherine recognized Charles at his side.

Handing his hat and coat to Fred, the old gentleman stepped into the salon and paused, looking around the room. Katherine went to meet him. He took both of her hands in his and kissed her lightly on the cheek.

"I'm sorry to be late, Katherine, but you can blame it on Charles. His plane was late."

"I'm just glad you're here," she smiled.

He turned and looked around the room again and Katherine asked eagerly, "How did I do? Is it like it used to be?" But her mind was asking why Charles was with him. What business did he have coming here now?

"Its beautiful, Katherine. You have done a magnificent job." Then as if he guessed her inner question, he added, "I needed Charles' signature on some of the final papers, and he was kind enough to volunteer to fly here to take care of it. He also wants to talk to you. I think you should listen to what he has to say, Katherine."

After a long pause she said a little grimly, "All right, if you think I should."

"I hope you don't mind my bringing him tonight?"

"Of course not," Katherine said politely, but untruthfully.

Charles came up just then and she greeted him formally, then ushered both men into the serving line.

Between eating her supper and seeing to the needs of her guests, she had no opportunity to find out what Charles wanted, but her mind was busy with speculation. Most of the diners had reached the dessert stage when Paul stood up and tapped his glass in the traditional bid for attention.

"Ladies and Gentlemen, I have an announcement to make."

The buzz of conversation died.

"I have the honor and pleasure," Paul continued a little pompously, "of announcing that Miss Dorothea Grant has consented to become Mrs. Paul Langhen. We haven't set the date yet, but it will be soon."

Katherine had been expecting this news for some time, but she hadn't known he planned to make the announcement at this party. Dorry's cheeks were pink and her eyes glowed with happiness.

Looking up, Katherine was startled to find Charles' gaze fixed intently on her face. Quickly turning away, she joined in the congratulations being offered to the engaged pair.

"How did you happen to choose this occasion for your announcement?" she asked Paul curiously.

Paul flushed like a teenager. "She said yes last night and I wasn't going to give her a chance to change her mind."

After dinner, the guests spread through the house. Some danced to the little three-piece orchestra in the corner of the salon. Even though it was now an empty gesture, Paul still encouraged a few to tour all the rooms. Later he told Katherine, "I could have sold the house three times in that one evening, but I'm glad the Senator was first. He made the highest offer."

Paul was surrounded by well-wishers and Dorothea was in demand as a dance partner. For Katherine it was a triumphant evening. She was praised and congratulated on every hand. Her success was almost frightening now that she knew how little she had been prepared for the job. With quiet poise she accepted the many compliments on the house. Secretly she felt that the greatest triumph was the new confident person she had built within herself.

Charles sat a little apart most of the time apparently waiting for a chance to talk to Katherine. Finally, he waylaid her coming out of the kitchen after settling with the caterer.

"Katy, Mr. Worthingham is ready to leave and I'm staying with him tonight. May I talk to you in the morning?"

"That would be best," she said without expression. "Make it about ten o'clock."

She said good night to the lawyer and watched them leave, wondering how Charles could have the nerve to face her. It had been two months since that New Year's Eve in California. He had said it was important that they talk, but she hadn't heard one single word from him in all this time. She couldn't imagine why he wanted to talk now.

It crossed her mind that he might regret parting with his inheritance now that he had learned it's real value. After all, he had gone straight to Mr. Worthingham. Also, now that she remembered, she never had received the divorce papers that Mark had asked about.

CHAPTER THIRTY-ONE

By ten o'clock the next morning Katherine was jumpy and impatient. When Charles arrived, she met him at the door wearing her coat.

"Let's go for a walk," she said briefly.

He paused in surprise. "It's pretty chilly out."

"I'm dressed for it." Her answer was curt and she set off determinedly for the woods.

Except for occasional evergreens the trees showed only bare sticks against the sky. In the shady places there were still small patches of snow from the last snowstorm. The ground was carpeted with damp leaves and melting ice edged the stream. Their breath frosted on the air. Katherine walked fast, both to warm her body and to calm her emotions. Charles followed her without saying anything. At last, warm and out of breath, she stopped beside one end of a huge old log that had fallen across the stream.

"All right," she said belligerently, "let's talk! What do you want?"

"First," Charles said quietly, "I brought you this." He pulled a folded manila envelope out of his pocket and handed it to her. "It's

the document on the divorce action. All you have to do is sign it and
the divorce will be final.”

It was stamped with a number of post office addresses and a
lot of arrows redirecting it from one to another for various reasons.
Finally 'Return to sender' was both stamped and handwritten across
everything else.

“They put the wrong address and its been traveling all over the
country or lying forgotten in some desk drawer for eight or nine
months,” he smiled. “I just got it back last week.”

“You could have mailed it again with the right address,” she
said without returning his smile. “Why are you here?”

“My signature was needed again on some of the papers when
you sold the house. And yes,” he held up his hand to stop her when
she opened her mouth, “I could have done that by mail, too. And, no,
I don’t want any part of the money! You earned every penny and it’s
yours! Katherine, I just want to explain about last New Year's Eve
and I certainly did not want to do that by mail!”

“That hardly needs explaining,” she said acidly. “I understand
about hormones, Charles.”

“Katherine, please! You said you would listen to me!”

“Yes, I did say that, didn’t I?” she mocked him. Folding her
arms angrily across her chest, she sat down on the end of the log.
“Okay, I’m listening!”

“In the first place, Katy, by the time you came back last fall I
had already begun to realize I had made a mistake, but I couldn’t
admit how big a fool I’d been. Betty was more interested in my
comfortable financial position than she was in me, but she flattered
the hell out of me, and I swallowed it whole.”

And I’d been ignoring you for a long time, Katherine thought
guiltily.

"She was also extremely jealous," he went on, "even of Mark and Fern. When you came back, she accused me of seeing you every time I went out of the house. Then the night I did see you at their house, we had a hell of a fight and she took off for her folks in Illinois."

"So then you figured you'd just come back to me, did you?"

"No. I figured our marriage was over. You know as well as I do, neither of us had been very happy for several years. You made it pretty clear you were enjoying your freedom and, right then, I wasn't sure I wanted to be married to anybody, either. I just thought we might be friends. A lot of divorced people are, you know."

"Friends?" Katherine looked up at him scornfully. "With bedroom privileges?"

"No, Katy. I never intended that and you know I didn't." Charles' face turned red and he seemed to have difficulty in trying to explain what he meant.

" It . . . the situation just got out of control before I knew it. I had realized how much I still cared the day we went Christmas shopping, but you froze me out pretty fast. Then that night I thought . . . I hoped it wasn't just the champagne . . . I thought you still cared. I was going to come back the next morning and find out if you were willing to try again . . . to see if we could work it out."

"Oh?" she said skeptically. "Well, why didn't you? You didn't say a word. You didn't even call to say good-bye!"

"Katy, I didn't know what to do. When I got home that night, Betty was there waiting for me. I knew she was back in town, but I'd been avoiding her. She said she was pregnant, and that I'd better marry her, or else! She was hysterical. She threatened to sue me or kill herself and our unborn baby. She was like a crazy person, Katy! I couldn't do anything with her. I didn't want to marry her but I couldn't deny my responsibility for the situation."

Serves you right, Katherine thought vindictively, but much of her anger faded as she heard the helplessness edge into his voice as he recounted that night. A very conservative, reserved man, Charles would have been totally demoralized at finding himself facing such a situation.

"Are you going to marry her?" she asked.

"No," he said quietly. "I would have. I felt I had to if there was to be a child, but she wasn't pregnant. Her menstrual period started about a week later. She claimed she was having a miscarriage. When I insisted on taking her to a doctor she admitted it was all an act to force me into marriage."

"When did all this happen?" Katherine asked suspiciously.

"About a week after you left," he said. He saw the quick anger flair in her face again and said quickly, "Wait a minute, let me finish."

"So, finish!" Katherine snapped

"I was so relieved to be out of the mess I'd created that I went straight to Fern and Mark and told them it had ended. I said I was going to see you that weekend and try to talk you into forgiving me. Mark told me it was too late for that."

"He said, 'Mom's in love with that real estate man who is handling the estate. She told Fern that she wasn't coming back because her future was in Maryland."

"But, I didn't . . . Katherine stopped as she remembered. She had told Fern her future was in Maryland, but she was referring to her career, not Paul.

"So, I didn't come. After what I'd done, I thought I had no right to interfere if you had built a new life for yourself. Then Mr. Worthingham called about the papers he wanted me to sign. He happened to mention that your real estate man was in love with your assistant. I had to come and see for myself what the situation really was.

"I don't know why I behaved the crazy way I did, Katherine. Suddenly I was afraid of getting old. Maybe it was this male menopause the psychiatrists talk about," he added. "I don't know. I do know I am deeply ashamed of hurting you. I love you, Katy. I had to know if there was any chance you might be willing to try again."

Katherine sat looking down, her thoughts in chaos. What did she really want? One thing she was certain of; she didn't want what her marriage had become in the last few years.

Out of the silence, Charles asked heavily, "Is there any chance at all for us?"

Katherine looked up into the anxious face. There was a little less hair and quite a few more wrinkles, but he was still a handsome man. The pain in his eyes touched her heart.

I still care, she thought in surprise. I still love him, but I don't know if that is enough.

She thought about the house. The successful restoration of life to a shell of wood and plaster had opened a fantastic vista of her future. She couldn't turn her back on that. It might not be possible to turn her back on Charles, either.

Tears blurred her vision. "I don't know. Everything's changed. I'm not the same person anymore. Our relationship could never be the same again."

"Does that mean you don't want to try again?" Charles was looking away across the field as if he were afraid he might see the death of his hope in her face.

"No. I just don't know. I'm all mixed up, Charles. I think I love you but I'm not sure that's enough. I need time to weigh the future. For your sake, as well as mine, I don't want to make a mistake."

He drew a deep breath as if he had been granted a temporary reprieve.

"All right, Katy. I won't push; I've made enough mistakes for both of us."

They walked back to the Gardiner house in silence. Charles went directly to his car. "Good-bye, Katy," he said as he slid under the wheel. "I'll be waiting for your call."

With a sense of loss Katherine watched the car move away from her down the long driveway. Tears streaked her cheeks.

"I don't want to make a mistake," she whispered as she turned to go in the house.

Dorothea was in her room packing clothes. When she heard footsteps in the hall she abandoned her task and met Katherine at the door. Sympathetically she observed Katherine's red-rimmed eyes and dejected air.

"Did Charles leave?" she asked although she had heard the car drive away.

Katherine nodded. "He's gone."

"I danced with him at the party last night. He seems awfully nice." She hesitated, afraid Katherine might resent her question "Can't. . .don't you. . .do you think you could ever forgive him?"

"It isn't that, everybody makes mistakes," Katherine mopped at a renewed flow of tears, "but I can't go back to that cage."

"What do you mean, cage?"

"I was trapped alone in that big house. The kids were gone. Charles was away all day. I had no training for anything. Day after day I watched TV or looked out the window to see what my neighbors were doing. When I tried to tell Charles how I felt he'd just hide behind his newspaper, or tell me to take up a hobby. I had sacrificed my career for him and he couldn't care less how unhappy I was."

There was a whining note in her voice and Dorothea was shocked.

"What did you expect him to do about it?"

"I don't know, but he just didn't care. His business was more important than I was. Instead of coming home he'd have dinner with some of his business friends or play golf all weekend.

This was a weak self-pitying woman Dorry had never seen. She felt as if her idol had betrayed her.

"Katherine Gardiner! I never would have expected you, of all people, to feel sorry for yourself. It's no wonder he found someone else. You must have been a ball to come home to!"

"Dorothea!" Katherine gasped. "How dare you talk to me that way?"

"What did he use; a key or a time lock?"

"What are you talking about?"

Dorry was looking squarely in Katherine's eyes as she said, "If a cage is not locked, a person can walk out of it any time he wants to,". . .she paused deliberately . . ."if he wants to. I assume Charles must have had you locked in."

"You don't know any thing about it, so just shut up!" Katherine was almost shouting she was so angry.

Tears filled Dorothea's eyes at this exposure of her idol's clay feet.

"Katherine, you have shown me a whole new world. I've watched you struggle with work almost beyond your strength and persist in spite of many setbacks. You have done a magnificent job transforming this house. Paul says that with a little more experience you'll be the best decorator he's ever seen. You have the intelligence, the talent and the strength to do anything, yet you sat there on your rump and felt sorry for yourself until you nearly ruined your life. Charles didn't put you in that cage, you did it to yourself."

Dorry's indictment struck Katherine with a force of understanding that seemed to knock the breath out of her for a second. In that instant she saw with painful clarity what had happened to her marriage and the view wasn't flattering. She'd been wallowing in self-pity that had closed her mind to anything but herself and excluded Charles from her life. He'd been an easy mark for Betty's attention and flattery. Her emotions churning, Katherine turned and started downstairs.

Glimpsing the devastation on her face, Dorothea called, "Katherine, wait, I'm sorry . . . "

"It's all right," Katherine interrupted her, "I just want to be by myself for a few minutes to think things out."

In the library there was a fire burning in the little fireplace. She supposed Fred had built it, although the furnace was keeping the house comfortable.

Katherine sank back in the little rocker seeking the same sense of sanctuary she had found the first night in this house. Awareness of her share of guilt in the destruction of her marriage filled her with shame.

As she gazed into the fire, the bright coals gradually turned to ash. Katherine imagined she could see a wrinkled old face with gray hair appear on the fire bed. She seemed to hear the voice of the old lady with the cane.

"It's the last time for yesterday, Katy. From tomorrow, there's no looking back and no more tears."

It just took me so long to learn what I was really crying about, she thought. I kept looking back, bemoaning the loss of my place as the center of my own little world when a whole new world was right there just outside my door. I locked it out and I locked Charles out, too.

"Are you all right, Katherine?" Dorothea asked from the library doorway.

Katherine heaved a great sigh as she rose from the little rocker. "Yes, finally I'm all right, Dorry. Can you help me pack? Charles is leaving on the afternoon plane, and I'm going to have to hurry if I plan on making it."

Happy tears suddenly shimmered in Dorry's eyes.

"You're going back to California?"

"Right. I think there's a cage out there that needs redecorating."

www.ingramcontent.com/pod-product-compliance
Lightning Source LLC
Chambersburg PA
CBHW030923120626
46554CB00001B/254